L
C

Marlene Suson

MILLS & BOON LIMITED
ETON HOUSE   18-24 PARADISE ROAD
RICHMOND   SURREY   TW9 1SR

*All the characters in this book have no existence outside
the imagination of the Author, and have no relation
whatsoever to anyone bearing the same name or names.
They are not even distantly inspired by any individual
known or unknown to the Author, and all the incidents
are pure invention.*

*All Rights Reserved. The text of this publication or any
part thereof may not be reproduced or transmitted in any
form or by any means, electronic or mechanical,
including photocopying, recording, storage in an
information retrieval system, or otherwise, without the
written permission of the publisher.*

*This book is sold subject to the condition that it shall not,
by way of trade or otherwise, be lent, resold, hired out or
otherwise circulated without the prior consent of the
publisher in any form of binding or cover other than that
in which it is published and without a similar condition
including this condition being imposed on the subsequent
purchaser.*

*First published in Great Britain 1989
by Mills & Boon Limited*

© Marlene Suson 1989

*Australian copyright 1989
Philippine copyright 1989
This edition 1989*

ISBN 0 263 76465 6

*Set in Times Roman 10½ on 12 pt.
04-8906-66899 C*

Made and printed in Great Britain

CHAPTER ONE

RETURNING from a late afternoon ride in Hyde Park, Viscount Vinson found his servants, under the flustered eye of his usually imperturbable butler, rushing about his elegant residence in Curzon Street as though calamity had struck in his absence.

Even more astonishing, Vinson's haughty valet, Swope, was actually carrying a portmanteau upstairs. Normally, Swope, who was considerably higher in the instep than his employer, would have been mortally affronted at the suggestion that he, rather than a lower servant, perform such a demeaning task.

When Vinson inquired of Boothe, his harassed butler, what had thrown his usually serene household into such turmoil, he was told 'The Earl arrived not above a half-hour ago.'

'Good God!' exclaimed the startled Viscount, immediately understanding the uproar. Even with advance warning of a visit, his demanding high stickler of a father always managed to turn the house upon its ear when he arrived. 'Why has he come?'

'As to that, I cannot say,' Boothe replied.

'Is my mother with him?'

Boothe's correct voice took on a woeful overtone. 'I fear he did not bring the Countess with him.'

Travelling without his wife was guaranteed to put the Earl of Bourn in a miff even if the journey did not. To the enormous relief of his servants, he rarely went anywhere without her.

An apprehensive frown marred the Viscount's usually amiable countenance. He must have done something that had put him in his father's black books. Nothing less than that would have induced Bourn, who disliked travelling as much as he disliked London, to make the tiresome journey to the city from his country seat in Suffolk—and without his wife.

Vinson's dark suspicion became a certainty when Boothe said, 'His lordship instructed that you are to go to him immediately in his apartments.'

The Viscount nodded, heartily wishing he had accepted the invitation to an exceedingly dull house party that would have put him at this very moment in Lancashire instead of London.

Sympathy showed in the butler's eyes as the Viscount, clad in buff riding-coat, leather boots by Hoby and buckskin breeches, turned towards the stairs. The young master was in for a trimming, if Boothe knew the Earl, and Boothe *did* know him, having been in his employ these past thirty-five years.

The young master was a relatively recent tenant of the Earl's London house. Eight months ago Ashley Neel, now Viscount Vinson, had succeeded to the title and the enormous expectations of his half-brother William on the latter's death in a curricle accident. His father had promptly insisted that Ashley's furnished rooms in George Street would no longer do. The future Earl must live at Bourn House.

The advent of this new resident had been a source of rejoicing among the servants. William, who had occupied the house for several seasons prior to his death, had been difficult to serve and impossible to please.

The half-brothers had been as different as night and day. William had favoured his late mother: serious, dutiful, and precise as a pin. Worse, he had been so full of his own consequence that he had been irritatingly pompous. Ashley, on the other hand, never took himself or much of anything else seriously. His easy manner and winning smile won him loyalty and quality of service from his inherited staff that would have astounded the late William.

Ashley had been gifted with his vivacious mother's charm, irrepressible humour, social grace and innate amiability. These blessings were coupled with a tall, muscular body, curly dark hair and arrestingly handsome face with laughing, vividly green eyes and a noble nose. This felicitous combination of personality and appearance guaranteed that no man's company was more coveted by shrewd hostesses and nubile young ladies of quality. Unfortunately for the latter's aspirations, however, he enjoyed a most agreeable connection with Sir Fletcher Roxley's lady, arguably the most beautiful woman in London, that had robbed him of any interest in acquiring a wife of his own.

The Viscount climbed the stairs for the interview with his father as eagerly as a condemned man mounts the Tyburn gallows. The relationship between the autocratic Earl and his son had been an uneasy one ever since, as an under-age youth, Ashley had tumbled wildly in love and tried in vain to marry without his father's approval.

When Ashley knocked at the Earl's apartments at the back of the house, his father's gruff voice bade him to enter without enquiring as to his identity. The Viscount steeled himself for the ordeal ahead.

To his surprise, he caught his normally impassive, ram-rod-straight father slumped wearily on a green bergère chair by a window that overlooked a small garden. The Earl looked so morosely unhappy and anxious that his son caught his breath. For a startled instant, Ashley wondered whether his father was dreading their impending interview as much as he was.

Seeing his son, the Earl instantly straightened. All definable emotion vanished from a face whose most arresting aspect was a pair of thick black brows that slanted diagonally downward, giving it a habitually disapproving cast.

The Viscount, forcing a smile to his lips, said lightly, 'What a pleasant surprise to find you here.'

'I doubt it,' Bourn said with his characteristic bluntness.

It was not an auspicious start, but his son persevered. 'What brings you on a surprise visit to London?'

'You, what else?' The Earl gestured impatiently for his son to take a second green bergère chair pulled up near his own. He was a large man, powerfully built, and as tall as his slimmer son, who stood well over six feet. But age had made inroads. His face was lined; his hair had thinned and whitened. Although his hazel eyes had lost none of their shrewdness, they seemed faded, making his peculiar brows all the more prominent.

As Ashley seated himself in the designated chair, his father said abruptly, 'Louisa gave birth to another girl two days ago.'

Louisa was the widow of Ashley's half-brother. Siring an heir had been the only thing that the estimable William had failed to do. Not that he had not tried. Dutiful as always, he had married the woman selected for him by his father and produced a half-dozen progeny—all girls. At his death, his wife was increasing for a seventh time, and it had been hoped that a son might be born to him posthumously. But now the baby was another daughter.

'I am sorry,' Ashley sympathised. 'I know how much you wanted it to be a boy.'

Since William's death, the Earl had become increasingly preoccupied with the succession. Should Ashley die without a male heir, both the earldom and the great fortune entailed with it would pass to Henry Neel, a distant cousin of dubious reputation, a possibily that revolted Ashley's father.

The Earl said sternly, 'You are eight and twenty, Ashley. It is long past time that you did your duty by marrying and producing sons. I shall not have Henry Neel inherit. William's killer will not benefit from his death.'

Ashley winced. He found it difficult to believe that his rakehell cousin, whatever his other failings, could be a murderer. Unlike William, who had loathed Henry with an unreasoning passion and cut him at every opportunity, Ashley had always been friendly with his cousin and had even lent him money on occasion. Although Henry had a wicked reputation with women and cards, he was also amusing, if overly cynical, and could be enormously charming. It was widely suspected, but never proved, that his remarkable success at cards was due to something other than luck. Having watched Henry play, Ashley had no doubt that his cousin was a cardsharp, but murder was quite a different matter.

Yet the Earl, normally the most rational of men, was not one to make wild accusations. 'Do you have new evidence indicating that Henry was responsible for William's death?' Ashley asked.

'No, but Henry won a great sum by betting against my son in that fatal curricle race. Furthermore, it was Henry who proposed it and coaxed William into participating. It was not at all like him to gamble.'

That was true enough. But William was so inordinately (and unjustifiably) proud of his ability with the ribbons that his hated cousin could easily have teased him into accepting a wager that he would defeat Charles Bence's new pair of greys.

During the race, a wheel on William's curricle had come off as he rounded a curve, throwing him from his perch. Initially, his injuries were not thought to be fatal, but while recuperating he was stricken with a congestion of the lungs, which killed him.

An examination of the wheel revealed that it had been tampered with, but an enquiry into the tragedy produced no answers as to who was responsible for the sabotage.

'I could readily believe that Henry might try to fix a race,' Ashley said, 'but I do not think him capable of murder.'

'Then you disappoint me,' his father said coldly. 'However, I did not come here to discuss Henry's guilt, but your lack of a wife.'

The Viscount, who was lounging carelessly in his bergère chair, stiffened. 'I fear blame for that lies with you, not me.' Although he spoke lightly, his voice had a harsh overtone. 'Had you not forbade it, I would have been married eight years ago to a lady who has since presented her lucky husband with three sons.'

'I forbade the woman, not the state.'

'But to me they were inseparably joined,' Ashley retorted. Eight years ago the beauteous Estelle Sutton had accepted Ashley's offer. He had adored her, but she had been of less than distinguished origins, and her profligate family had not a feather to fly with. Her father, knowing her to be his only asset, had insisted on a very large sum from Bourn in return for her hand. The Earl had flatly refused to pay it or to have Estelle as a daughter-in-law.

Ashley, who had been under-age, would have defied his father by eloping with her to Gretna Green. But on learning that Bourn would cut off his second son without a penny if he married her, Estelle withdrew her acceptance and instead married Sir Fletcher Roxley, twenty years her senior but reputed to be the wealthiest man in London.

The broken-hearted Ashley was so unhappy and bitter about his father, whom he blamed for his loss of Estelle, that it was weeks before he could be induced to enter the Earl's company again. It took all of the Countess's great charm and persuasiveness to reconcile her son to her husband, but even after she succeeded, the relationship remained strained.

Although Ashley loved his father and had long since come to regret the breach between them, the fierce, formidable Earl was not the kind of man either to express or to receive such sentiments. As the years passed, Ashley became increasingly certain that he was a bitter disappointment to his father.

After Estelle's marriage, Ashley had tried in vain to forget her with a series of high fliers, but none of these beauties had succeeded in making him do so. Nor had any of the marriage-minded diamonds of the first water who had cast lures for him managed to win his heart. These incomparables and the birds of paradise who had been in his protection had all suffered from the same defect: they had cordially bored him after a few weeks.

Ashley's father said bitterly, 'Now you have taken up with Estelle again.'

The startled Vicsount wondered how his father had learned of the affair. Not that it was much of a secret, he concluded ruefully. He had attempted to be discreet for the lady's sake, but she had shown no such inclination. Sir Fletcher Roxley had proven to be as disagreeable and boring as he was rich. After providing him with three sons, his wife had considered her marital duties fully discharged and looked elsewhere for romance. Discovering that her first love had matured into one of the most sought-after, sophisticated bachelors in London, she determined to recapture him, and succeeded.

'Since Estelle is safely married, you have no cause to worry,' Ashley told his father.

'But you are not! Nor do you show any inclination to become so, with her back in your life. If you wish to spare me worry, you will take a wife.'

'There is no woman that I wish to marry.'

'Then your wishes be damned!' his father said impatiently. 'It is your duty to marry a wife worthy of the honour of being Countess of Bourn, and to do so immediately.'

With difficulty, Ashley concealed his own rising temper behind an ironic rejoinder. 'I fear I cannot think of a single young lady worthy of so great an honour.'

'I expected just such an answer,' the Earl said with the air of a man whose darkest suspicions have been vindicated. He drew a paper from the inside pocket of his coat and waved it at Ashley. 'That is why I have drawn up a list of seven young ladies who are acceptable.'

His son stared at the paper in disbelief. 'I am no longer an under-age youth whom you can command to do what you wish!'

To Ashley's surprise, his father did not respond in his usual autocratic manner. Instead he said unhappily, 'It is not my intention to command you to do anything, and indeed I am not. The last thing on earth that I wish is to open another breach between us. But I am asking—indeed, begging—you to marry.'

The Viscount was much moved by the Earl's conciliatory manner and his dread of another estrangement, a dread that was shared equally by his son. Ashley realised that he had been correct in his initial impression that his father hated this confrontation as much as he did.

'If William's baby had been a boy, I would not force the issue now, but it is your duty as heir to marry and sire sons. I beg you to meet your responsibility by choosing one of these young ladies.' The Earl again waved his list at Ashley. 'You must save your family the disgrace of having the title fall into Henry's hands.'

'What of Estelle?' Ashley asked quietly.

'Why you would want to plough another man's field is beyond me,' the Earl said bluntly. 'But so long as you marry and produce sons, I don't care if she remains your mistress until you die.'

'I doubt that my wife would be so complaisant,' Ashley said wryly. 'There, Papa, is the difficulty, for I do not intend to give Estelle up.'

'Then arrange a marriage with a sensible woman of breeding who understands such things,' his father counselled. Seeing the revolted look on Ashley's face, he continued hastily, 'I know what I am asking of you, for I, too, married once for duty. My father chose William's mother for me, yet ours was a satisfactory union.'

'But not nearly so happy as your second with Mama,' Ashley guessed. Despite the great difference in his parents' ages and personalities, their love and devotion to each other had remained untarnished through the years.

The Earl's faded hazel eyes brightened at the mention of his wife. 'I won't try to gammon you. My marriage to your mama has been far happier than my first was.'

'And that is why I want to marry a woman I love,' Ashley said quietly.

'But I fear you will never love any woman but Estelle,' the Earl said sadly, suddenly looking very tired. 'Perhaps it was a mistake to have prevented you from marrying her. I know you think I did so because she lacked breeding and money, but it was because I thought her a selfish creature whose first affection would always be for herself. I feared that she would make you very unhappy.'

'Estelle loved me as much as I loved her,' Ashley exclaimed angrily.

'Did she?' his father asked sceptically, rubbing his forehead wearily with his fingers. 'You were so young then that I thought you would soon forget her, but clearly I was wrong. Not one of all the beauties who have dangled after you has been able to capture your heart. I must say that your taste in women, whether flirts or convenients, is dazzling.'

Shocked, Ashley exclaimed, 'I thought you had no inkling of my ladybirds.'

'Of course I knew of them,' Bourn said impatiently. 'Everything involving you is of great concern to me.'

'Why?' Ashley asked bitterly. 'Afraid I'll disgrace the family?'

'Not at all.' Again the Earl rubbed his hand wearily over his eyes. When he spoke, there was a plaintive note in his voice that Ashley had never heard before. 'Your mama misses you dreadfully. It would give her so much pleasure if you would visit us at Winton more frequently.'

Ashley seldom went there because he was uncertain of how welcome he was to his father. 'And you, Papa,' he asked, determined to know the truth, 'would you like me to visit?'

'What a corkbrained question! I should like nothing better!' The Earl's voice was thick with emotion. The list of names fell unnoticed from his left hand. 'May God and poor William forgive me, but you always were my favourite. So like your dear mama.'

'*What?*' This emotional confession from his usually impassive father stunned the Viscount.

'Of course, I tried very hard to hide it, especially when William was alive. It is quite unworthy for a man to have favourites among his children.'

'Oh, Papa!' Ashley exclaimed in a choked voice. All those years when he had thought . . . He bent over hastily, fumbling with the paper that his father had dropped in order to cover the emotion that overcame him. When he looked up, his green eyes were very bright indeed. So were the Earl's.

His father's passionate confession had a singular effect on Ashley. In that moment he would have tried to fly to the moon if the Earl had asked it of him. He turned his attention to his father's list of prospective brides with the air of a man who knows his duty and is determined to do it.

Bourn said anxiously. 'All the marriages this past year sadly decimated the ranks of desirable young ladies, but all seven are of excellent breeding. And that snake Henry cannot be permitted to succeed to what I, and my father and grandfather before me, spent our lives building.'

Vinson had to agree that if his father's suspicions of Henry were true, it was unthinkable that he should do so. Even if they were not, such a loose screw as Henry was not a fit successor to the long line of distinguished men who had held the title.

Despite, or, perhaps more accurately, because of, his determination to honour his father's wish that he marry, Ashley contemplated the list with dismay. He knew six of the seven young ladies, and his father was right. It was a very poor year to be bride-picking.

Lady Margaret White, who headed the list, was exquisitely lovely—and exquisitely boring.

Grace and Jane Kelsie, daughters of the Marquess of Levisham's late younger brother, were also acknowledged beauties who had made a joint London come-out last season. They had been very forward in signalling their interest in Ashley, but they had both struck him as tiresome creatures who hid an ill-tempered nature behind a sugared manner. He suspected that once married they would display an alarming tendency to become as shrewish and domineering as their overbearing mama.

Elizabeth Trott, at twenty-five the oldest on the Earl's list, had been the Incomparable of her first London season. She had kept hordes of suitors dangling, preferring the adulation of many men to the wedding ring of one. But that had been seven years ago. Now she had grown plump and faded, trying to conceal beneath a liberal application of paint and powder that she was no longer a beauty. Her many admirers had vanished with her beauty, but even at the height of her popularity Ashley had not been one of them.

Mary Milbank was of superior breeding and fortune but far below the others in beauty, and missish in the bargain.

Of the six young ladies on the list that he knew, Emily Picton was by far the best of the lot, combining beauty and a lively personality. He might even have been willing to offer for her had not his good friend, Mercer Corte, been wildly in love with her.

Ashley knew nothing of Lady Caroline Kelsie, the final name on the list, but supposed her to be Levisham's daughter.

The Earl, watching his son's face anxiously, said, 'What do you think of the young ladies?'

'I do not know Lady Caroline Kelsie,' Ashley replied evasively, looking out at a magnificent magnolia tree in the garden. It was in full flower, its big blooms creamy against the glistening green leaves.

'Nor is she known to me, but she is of most distinguished parentage,' Bourn said.

'I collect she must be the Marquess of Levisham's daughter.'

'Yes, and her mother was the most enchanting creature I have ever known, except for your own dear mama. How poor Levisham adored her, but she died very young. He was so heartbroken that he retired from society, living as a recluse at Bellhaven.'

'Apparently he is returning to society, for I have been invited to Bellhaven for a spot of shooting and angling. I was astonished by the invitation, since I have never met the Marquess.'

'Levisham wrote to me, too. Before his wife died, we were good friends, but I have not heard from him in years. Until his letter, I was not even aware that his son died nearly two years ago of a putrid sore throat. Now he has only his daughter left.'

'Will you be going to Bellhaven, too?' Ashley asked.

The Earl shook his head. 'No, Levisham wrote to tell me why he had invited you.'

'Why did he?'

'He is trying to matchmake. He was very candid—he wants to see his daughter married and settled. I am honoured that he considers you as a possible son-in-law.'

Ashley, not feeling in the least honoured, asked, 'Why is it that I have not seen his daughter in London?'

'She does not come out until next season.'

'Surely you cannot wish me to marry a child scarcely out of the schoolroom?' Ashley cried, aghast at the thought.

'She is a trifle young,' the Earl conceded. 'But if she is as much like her marvellous mama as Levisham says, that won't signify. Not even Georgiana, Duchess of Devonshire, could hold a candle to her.'

'So legend has it.'

'For once legend is correct. What a delight the Marchioness was. She would say the most outrageous things, yet she was the kindest-hearted creature imaginable. And a great heiress in the bargain. Her fortune, by the way, was bequeathed to her daughter.' A teasing glint shone in the Earl's eyes. 'So you need not worry that Lady Caroline might marry you only for your money.'

'How comforting,' Ashley said drily. 'If the girl is such a paragon, why is Levisham trying to marry her off before she has her first season?'

'That is for you to find out. Furthermore, four of the other young ladies on my list will also be at Bellhaven.'

'You cannot know how I abhor matchmaking parties,' Ashley said with loathing.

His father smiled sympathetically. 'I dare say that I do, but there is no better shooting and fishing anywhere in England than at Bellhaven. It will relieve you to know that several of the kingdom's most eligible bachelors, including Lord Sanley, have also been invited.' The quizzing glint reappeared in the Earl's eyes. 'The young ladies will have so many to choose from that you may find yourself ignored.'

'I pray that may be the case,' his son said fervently.

CHAPTER TWO

ASHLEY, driving his racing curricle with the skill that had justly made him a famous whipster, had left behind his entourage of travelling-coach, baggage, groom, valet, and even his indignant tiger, who had predicted with less truth than wishful thinking that his master could not manage his high-stepping pair of chestnuts without him.

A brief, heavy rain had left the road to Bellhaven spotted with puddles. The leaves of the oak and chestnut trees were beaded with water. Rolling fields, lushly green in the rain's wake, were decorated with golden patches of ragwort. Creamy honeysuckle and pink dog-rose poked from hedgerows, and delicate blue harebells were scattered along the roadside.

The Viscount had wanted this solitary ride through the pretty countryside to sort out his troubled thoughts. By now he had reluctantly reconciled himself to the necessity, although not the desirability, of marrying. Titles carried with them obligations, and it was his duty as heir to the earldom to marry and produce children. He had always hoped for a love match, but his father was right. At eight and twenty years, after years of having found the marriage mart's finest offerings wanting, he was unlikely to fall hopelessly in love again as he had with Estelle. Since he must make a loveless marriage sooner or later, he thought gloomily, it might as well be sooner and set his father's mind at ease.

Ashley was much troubled, too, about the possibility that Henry Neel could have been involved in William's death. There had been bad blood between the two cousins for as long as Ashley could remember, and their hatred had intensified with the years. William, the high stickler, had regarded Henry's scandalous career at the gaming tables and in the boudoir as an unforgivable blot on the Neel family honour, and had let him know it at every opportunity. Henry, in turn, had delighted in goading the humourless William into a fury whenever he could.

Ashley was positive that the key to William's death was an evil-looking man that his good friend, Mercer Corte, had seen near Bourn House early on the morning of William's race. Corte had been returning home, a few doors down from Bourn House in Curzon Street, at about four a.m. when a hulking figure, moving with astonishing quietness for a man of his size, had emerged from the path that led to the Bourn stable.

'I knew immediately that he could be up to no good,' Mercer had told Ashley later. 'I've never seen an uglier-looking blackguard. His right ear was missing. He had two ugly scars on his face, one on his forehead and the other down his left cheek, and his nose was flattened. He was clearly a man who belonged in the rookeries of St Giles, not Curzon Street.'

Ashley was certain that the one-eared man must have been the one who had tampered with the wheel of William's curricle, but had he been hired to do so by Henry? To answer that question, Ashley would have to locate the man among the tens of thousands crowded into London's slums, a virtual impossibility if one did not know where to begin looking.

Ashley's equipage reached the high iron gates of Bellhaven. A stout porter hurried out of his stone cottage, which was half covered with ivy. The Viscount wondered whether his lack of attendants and baggage would appear suspicious enough for the gatekeeper to deny him entrance. But the man merely said, 'Ay, and ye must be Lord Vinson.'

'How did you know?' the surprised Ashley asked.

'Ye be a day late. The others came yesterday. Only other body 'pected today be his lordship's solicitor.' The porter cast an appraising eye over Ashley's quietly elegant attire and expensive rig. 'And ye be no solicitor.' The man swung wide the gates so that Ashley could drive through them. 'This road takes ye to the house, but it be a fair piece.'

Ashley urged his horses up a broad avenue, lined with linden trees, that wound through Bellhaven's park. As he drove, he considered again his father's list of marital eligibles. Neither Lady Margaret White nor Elizabeth Trott would be at Bellhaven. But the beautiful Kelsie sisters, Mary Milbank and Emily Picton would. The first three held no attraction for him, and Emily Picton was spoken for. That left only the Marquess's daughter Caroline, and Ashley had come by default to pin great hopes on this unknown young lady, basing his optimisim on her papa's report that she was much like her mother.

By all accounts, the late, legendary Marchioness had been the most outrageous and captivating of beauties. Talk of her had revived in recent days with word that Levisham, after mourning her in solitude all these years, was at last inviting guests to Bellhaven again.

There was much curiosity about her daughter and only surviving child, but nothing was known about

Lady Caroline. She had been hidden away with her father at Bellhaven all of her life, and none of the ton had set eyes upon her. But it was universally agreed that if she favoured her mother she would be ravishing—and a great catch. No wonder that every eligible bachelor who had been invited to Bellhaven with Ashley had accepted.

Ashley's own curiosity about Lady Caroline, born of desperation, had reached a high pitch, and he could hardly wait to see her. Although he was badly put off by the thought of a bride out of the schoolroom, he grimly reminded himself that she would grow older. If only she would not turn out to be a dead bore.

Turning his attention to Bellhaven's park, which was as lovely as his father had said, Ashley slowed his chestnuts to a walk. Green glades and thick woods of beech, sycamore and oak spread over rolling hills. When the winding avenue topped a hill, Ashley saw in the distance Bellhaven's splendid north front glistening in the bright sun, its great portico's columns and triangular pediment freshly washed by the rain.

Seeking a better view of the mansion and its lovely setting, Ashley stopped his horses, jumped down from his curricle and made his way to a high knoll crowned by a solitary oak. What a magnificent view of Bellhaven he would have from that tree, he thought as he strode towards it. Its massive trunk was gnarled and thickened with age. Heavy branches, low to the ground, twisted off from the main trunk to form inviting crooks for a man who in his youth had been an accomplished tree-climber. Ashley was sorely tempted to see how much of his skill, unused for years, he had retained.

Staring up through the veil of green leaves, he discovered to his profound astonishment that the tree was already occupied. Dainty little feet, shod in muddy half-boots that peeked from beneath a faded blue skirt, were balancing precariously on one of the upper notches.

'What the devil are you doing up there?' he demanded.

His rough question caused the girl to start violently. She lost her balance and grabbed at a branch to steady herself, sending a miniature shower of waterdrops from the leaves, still wet from the earlier rain, cascading down on Ashley. Her hand missed the branch and caught instead a slender subsidiary that promptly broke away, and she fell.

Ashley had the presence of mind to put out his arms, and a wisp of a girl tumbled into them. The force of her fall brought Ashley to one knee, but he did not drop her.

For a moment they stared at each other, too surprised to speak. Her face, which seemed to be all huge grey eyes, reminded him of an elf. He judged her to be about thirteen. Her thin, boyish body as yet offered only a hint of the woman she would become. Her complexion was too brown and her face was too thin to be pretty. These defects were accentuated by the way she wore her long brown hair carelessly caught up in a knot atop her head. Several strands had escaped and curled incorrigibly about her head. The bedraggled skirt of her old calico gown bore the unmistakable imprint of several very muddy paws.

He restored her feet to the ground. Rising from his knee, he discovered that the child did not even reach his shoulder. He wondered whether she was a homeless waif who had taken refuge in the tree. Certainly she looked like one.

'You so startled me that I lost my balance,' she said indignantly.

He was nonplussed by her genteel, educated voice, which was at such variance with her impoverished appearance. 'My apologies, but I was equally startled to find a girl in the tree. Are you hurt?'

His question only served to increase her indignation. 'Of course not!' Her great grey eyes flashed dangerously. 'I am not so cowhearted as that. It is not the first tree that I have fallen out of.'

Ashley, more accustomed to girls who would swoon at the thought of climbing a tree, was so bemused by her reply that it took him a moment to recollect his duty as an Older Person to warn her of the danger of her ways. 'If you continue to tumble out of trees, you most likely will break your pretty little neck.'

'My neck isn't pretty,' she contradicted. 'My aunt says it is as scrawny as a chicken's.'

Ashley, startled by such self-deprecating candour, examined the offending creature and concluded that her aunt did it an injustice. It was, in fact, long and rather elegant, ending at a pretty little chin. She had some good points, taken individually, including a charming button of a nose and a sweet mouth. 'You do not seem cast down by your aunt's criticism,' he observed.

'I do not tease myself with what I cannot change.'

The eminent good sense of these words caused Ashley to reassess this odd little creature. She wanted conduct, but he could not help admiring her spirit. Her voice still puzzled him, though. It was too genteel to be that of the common servant or poor rustic's daughter that her clothes indicated. The unhappy thought that she might be a runaway struck him, and he asked, rather more sharply than he intended, 'Who are you?'

'Caro,' she replied as though no other identification were necessary. 'Who are you?'

Annoyed that she had not seen fit to disclose her surname, he responded curtly, 'Ashley.'

Inspecting his green double-breasted coat, one of Weston's masterpieces that more than made up in quiet elegance what it lacked in ostentation, Caro decided, 'You must be the new solicitor. I heard that you were to come today.'

Although startled at being mistaken for a solicitor, Ashley, who had never been puffed up with his own consequence, was amused rather than insulted. He doubted, however, that Weston would have been quite so unforgiving. 'You are not so astute as the gate-keeper,' he remarked with a grin.

The big grey eyes were puzzled. 'I beg your pardon, Mr Ashley?'

'It is not Mr Ashley,' he explained, deciding that she must be the daughter of one of Levisham's retainers. 'Ashley is my given name. My family name is Neel.' Since she clearly thought him a hireling of Levisham's and therefore her social equal, he would not embarrass her by using his title.

'No doubt you wonder what I was doing in that tree,' she said.

He grinned knowingly. 'Not at all. The view from it must be well worth the climb.'

She visibly warmed to him. 'Indeed it is. That is why it is one of my favourite spots.' Bequeathing him a smile that lit her little face in a beguiling mix of mischief and innocence, she announced warmly, 'I like you.'

'I am honoured,' Ashley said gravely. He gestured towards his curricle. 'May I offer you a ride?'

'Oh, yes,' she cried enthusiastically. 'Those are prime cattle you drive. What I should not give to have a pair like that!' Before he could help her, she dashed to his curricle and clambered up.

When he joined her on the seat, she instructed, 'Follow the avenue, and we will come to my home.'

As they trotted along, she proved to be far more impressed by his driving skill than she had been by Weston's coat, proclaiming him a regular out-and-outer.

'I wager that you would put that odious Paul Coleman in the shade even though you have not filed your teeth to points, as he has, to ape coachmen,' Caro said. 'He says it is all the crack to do so, but I think it crackbrained.'

Which aptly described the son and heir of Sir Thomas Coleman, Ashley thought with twitching lips. Poor Paul had far more blunt than brains.

'And he is a frightful braggart, too, about what a top sawyer he is with the ribbons, but he is not nearly so odious as Lord Sanley, who pinches maids' bottoms!'

Startled, Ashley looked at her sharply. 'Did he pinch your bottom?'

'No, he would not dare, for I am Levisham's daughter,' she said cheerfully, apparently not in the least offended at having been mistaken for a servant.

Ashley's head spun round, and he jerked the reins in his surprise. His horses, mistaking this for a command, stopped, but the Viscount did not notice.

His startled eyes stared at the thin brown face with the long, unruly wisps of hair fluttering about it and at the tiny, childish body in the faded, paw-stained old gown. For the first time in recent memory, Ashley's breeding and polished address failed him, and he blurted, 'Good lord, you cannot be Lady Caroline Kelsie!'

CHAPTER THREE

CARO'S elfin face puckered for an instant, and Ashley knew he had wounded her with the unintended insult that had been startled from him. But she recovered before he did, saying with a little smile that did not hide the pain in the big grey eyes, 'Yes, I am she. Quite shocking, is it not?'

In truth it was, but only because Ashley, in his wishful thinking, had endowed her with perfection. Now, having seen her, he longed to turn the curricle about and return immediately to London. There was no way on earth he would ever offer for her.

Nor would his father want him to. The Viscount's lips tightened in unhappy contemplation of the horror with which the Earl, who held such exalted notions of who would be an acceptable future Countess of Bourn, would react to this strange little waif.

Nevertheless, it had been most unforgivably rude of Ashley to have hurt her with his faux pas. Trying to smooth it over, he said hastily, with his most winning smile, 'Not shocking, only surprising. I have never before had the pleasure of a lady of rank tumbling out of a tree into my arms.'

'I am sure it was no pleasure, and I am not a lady,' she said matter-of-factly. 'Aunt Olive says I shall never be one, even though the title is mine by courtesy of birth. I fear that she is right, too. I am always saying and doing things a lady should not.' Caro's eyes were suddenly defiant. 'The truth is, I do not want to be

29

a lady. I have not the smallest interest in feminine accomplishments. I don't care a button for setting a fine stitch or singing prettily, which would be impossible in any event because I cannot carry a tune. And I am too plain-spoken to flatter eligible young men and to flirt with my useless fan. You cannot conceive how excessively tiresome being a lady is.'

Ashley, striving to keep his expression grave, said sympathetically, 'Now that you have explained it to me, I can see how it might be.'

'And it is worse now that we have guests. It is so unfair. While the men go out riding or play billiards, I and the other females are relegated to the morning-room. Not that they mind. But I do!'

'Surely you would not care for billards.'

The grey eyes flashed. 'I am an excellent player, good enough to beat Papa half the time! But Aunt Olive has banned me from the billiard-room while we have guests because she says ladies of the first respectability do not enter such premises. Why, I ask you, should ladies not enjoy the same pleasures as men? It is excessively unfair!'

Ashley, despite quivering lips, agreed solemnly, 'Indeed it is, Lady Caroline.'

'Pray, do not call me that! I hate it! Not only am I not a lady, but no one calls me Caroline except my aunt and her daughters.'

In his preoccupation with his unconventional companion, Ashley had quite forgotten his horses, and they had taken advantage of their master's inattention by stopping. Belatedly realising this, he urged them on.

As the curricle rolled forward, Caro confided. 'This has been the most wretched summer of my life. Aunt

Olive, for all she says it is impossible, is determined to turn me into a proper young lady like her daughters, and I have been prohibited from doing *everything* I like.'

He smiled gently at her woebegone countenance. 'Surely not everything?'

'Everything,' she said vehemently. 'I am not allowed to ride bareback or to climb trees or to swim in the river. I cannot even walk in the park unless I am accompanied by a footman!' Her voice rose indignantly. 'A footman, when I know every nook of Bellhaven better than anyone except Papa! Have you ever heard such nonsense?'

'How very vexing,' Ashley agreed, a glint of laughter in his eyes. Lady Caro might be a hopeless ineligible for marriage, but her candid conversation delighted him. 'I do not, however, recall a footman attending you in the tree.'

Caro laughed, a light, melodious little trill that Ashley found charming. When her grey eyes were alight with laughter and mischief, as they were now, they were quite beautiful.

'What an exceptional child you are,' he observed.

The laughter immediately faded from her face, and she drew herself up indignantly. 'I am not a child. I am seventeen.'

He started to speak, but she cut him off. 'I know I do not look it. I am so small. You cannot conceive what a trial it is to have to look up to everyone you talk to except children. Sometimes I think my neck shall have a permanent crick in it. I should so like to be tall and willowy like Emily Picton, but I fear I never shall be. My mama was tiny, and Papa says I take after her. Except that I don't really, for she was very beautiful, and I will never be beautiful either.'

Ashley looked at Caro's wistful little face. It was quite taking when it was animated. She might never be beautiful, but with guidance on how to accentuate her good points, she could be very striking.

'I think you will be very pretty, though,' he consoled her.

'What a hum!' she scoffed. 'My eyes are too big, my face is too thin and my complexion is too brown.'

'But you have a charming little nose and chin and a delightful mouth, especially when you smile,' Ashley said, carefully enumerating her good points.

'Are you telling me a whisker, or do you truly think so?' she asked eagerly.

He was moved by her obvious pleasure at his compliment. 'I truly think so,' he said gently, unconsciously reaching out to brush away a long brown strand of hair that had drifted over her face. Its texture was as fine as silk. No wonder it was so flyaway.

'My worst fault is my tongue,' she confessed. 'My aunt says I must always say whatever pops into my head no matter how outrageous it is, and she is right, but I cannot seem to help it. She blames it on my having lived such an isolated life with Papa. He is a recluse, you know. Aunt Olive insisted that Papa invite guests here this summer so that I could be exposed to other young people in society and learn how I should speak and act.' Her eyes grew thoughtful. 'At least that is what she told Papa, but I think her real reason was to try to catch husbands for Grace and Jane—those are her daughters.'

Ashley smiled, suspecting that Caro had read her aunt's motives rather better than that overbearing lady would have liked. He observed gently, 'Clearly you have not yet learned to curb your tongue.'

'It is very hard,' she confessed woefully, 'and now Aunt Olive has decreed that I must do so while our guests are here.' She gave a lugubrious sigh. 'I do not know how I shall manage that.'

'Nor I,' Ashley said with amusement. 'What prompted such an onerous decree?'

'Two things, neither of which merited such an edict,' Caro replied heatedly. 'Lord Sanley behaved shockingly to Meg, one of our maids, and she threatened to complain to Papa. He had the audacity to tell her that if she dared do so, he would see that she was turned out without a reference! The poor thing was terrified. She is only sixteen. I found her crying her heart out in a linen-closet and made her tell me what was wrong. I was so angry that when I saw Sanley at dinner last night, I told him that if he dared to bother her again, it was he who would be turned out!'

Ashley strove heroically against succumbing to the laughter that threatened to overwhelm him. What he would have given to have seen Sanley's face when he received Caro's ultimatum. Vinson doubted that his lordship, the Duke of Upton's heir, had ever before been called to task over his well-known propensity for lechery among the lower orders. Sanley's claim as Ashley's chief rival for the title of prime catch on the marriage mart rested on his enormous expectations rather than on any inherent charm. Although he was handsome enough, he was notoriously high in the instep and never put himself out to be pleasant.

Caro complained, 'It seems to me exceedingly unjust that it should be I, rather than he, who is sunk below reproach.'

'True,' Ashley responded gravely. 'It was Sanley who did the pinching.'

Caro smiled approvingly. 'I knew that you were a man of superior understanding.'

His superior understanding led Ashley to query tactfully. 'What other insignificant thing put you in your elders' black books?'

'Well,' she confessed, 'I heard this dreadful creaking when we were all together in the drawing-room after dinner last night. I was seated on a settee next to Sir Percival Plymtree, who was going on at great length about the most recent party at Carlton House.'

'He would,' Ashley muttered. Sir Percival, said to be the second wealthiest man in the kingdom after Sir Fletcher Roxley, was an incessant name-dropper and a malicious gossip. Considering himself top of the trees, Sir Percival was notorious for his extravagant dress and toilet. No man wore more ostentatious colours, fabrics and jewels or higher heels than Sir Percival, who was short in stature. Although a corpulent fop, he considered his physique excellent. Determined to maintain this fiction, he laced himself in with a determination that made Ashley wonder how he could still breathe.

'I was excessively perplexed by the creaking,' Caro said. 'Then it occured to me that I heard it whenever Sir Percival leaned forward, which he must do, for he wears such excessively high, stiff collars that he cannot bend his neck. At last, I asked him what was causing that strange creaking. He replied quite uncivilly that I was imagining it.' Indignation kindled in her grey eyes. 'I knew very well that I was not! So I pointed it out whenever it occurred. And he was finally forced to confess that he was wearing a corset. Can you imagine, a corset?' she asked, clearly scandalised. 'I thought that only women were foolish enough to torture themselves so. When I told him that, he got excessively red, indeed, rather purple in the face, and informed me that his is a *Cumberland* corset, identical to the one the Prince Regent wears. I was never so shocked. Our ruler wears a corset!'

Ashley lost his battle to maintain his sobriety and dissolved into uncontrollable laughter.

'I am happy that you find it amusing, for Sir Percival and Papa did not, and my cousins and Mary Milbank acted excessively shocked.' Her little face was suddenly perplexed. 'Though why they should I do not understand, for when none of the men was about, they said worse things about him. I believe that if one is not willing to say something to another's face, one should not say it behind his back!'

'A highly laudable but uncommon sentiment,' Ashley said drily. As uncommon as Caro herself. Levisham's house party, thanks to his daughter, promised to be far more entertaining than Ashley could have imagined.

Caro's head drooped. 'Now Aunt Olive says that I have sunk myself beneath reproach in the eyes of our guests and, worse, that I have mortified Papa.' She frowned in dismay. 'I would not do that for the world.'

'Of course you would not,' Ashley smoothed, 'and I would wager that your papa understands that.'

'Do you think so?' she asked, brightening.

'I do,' he assured her.

They rode quietly through a wood of beech and oak, with leaves occasionally dripping on to the curricle's occupants, but Caro seemed not to notice.

'What is your dog's name?' Ashley asked.

Her eyes widened in surprise. 'How did you know I had a dog?'

He glanced in the direction of her skirt.

Looking down, Caro brushed hastily at the muddy paw-prints on it. 'Dandie was excessively happy to see me this morning,' she explained. 'Aunt Olive banished him to the stable until our guests leave, and the poor thing is so lonely there. Do you like dogs?'

'Yes.'

Her eyes gleamed approvingly. 'I knew that you would. I wish you were one of our guests. You are far more interesting than any of them.'

'I am flattered. How did you decide that I was not a guest?'

'You have no baggage and no servants,' she replied promptly. 'All the men arrived with valet, groom, and at least one travelling-trunk. Besides, your coat is too modest.'

Ashley thought ruefully of the extortionate sum he had paid Weston for his 'modest' coat.

'Although, in truth,' Caro continued thoughtfully, 'I much prefer the way you dress. Both Sir Percival and Lord Sanley look excessively ridiculous in their high, stiff collars with points that threaten their eyes. And they spend *hours* tying their neckcloths. Papa says that they go through so much linen in trying to tie them properly that he may have to hire another laundress.'

'Have any of your elegantly-dressed guests captured your fancy?'

Caro looked at him as if he were an escapee from a lunatic asylum. 'No, nor I theirs, but it does not signify, for I plan to devote myself to Papa and never marry. Which is just as well, for I am sure no man would want to wed a plain little stick like myself, except perhaps for my fortune.'

Self-deprecating young ladies who voluntarily rejected marriage were as rare in Ashley's experience as those who climbed trees, and he asked curiously, 'Why do you hold marriage in such particular aversion that you want to become an ape-leader?'

'Why are spinsters called that?' she enquired. 'I asked Papa once, but he said he did not know.'

'It is said that their punishment after death for failing to increase and multiply is to lead apes through hell.' He grinned at her. 'So beware of what fate awaits you. Surely it would be better to marry?'

'You are quizzing me. I don't believe such nonsense, and you don't either.'

'No, of course not,' he admitted, 'but what has given you such a distaste for marriage?'

'A woman has no rights once she is married. They are as helpless as Sanley thought poor Meg would be against his word. Everything a wife has becomes her husband's to control, even her children. It is excessively unjust.'

The curricle emerged from the damp shade of the woods into the bright sunshine where a quarter of a mile ahead of them Bellhaven sparkled in the light.

Caro turned her eyes, hot with outrage, towards Ashley. 'I shall not place myself at the mercy of a husband who may turn out to be a drunkard like Mr Burk, who is always in his cups. Or a wastrel like Sir John Wesley, who lost his estate and his wife's fortune at the gaming table. Or a brute like Mr Potter, who beats his poor Clara even though she is the sweetest little thing. Then there is Amelia Coleberd, who brought a great dowry to her clutch-fisted husband and is required to dress herself and her children in hand-me-downs that she begs from her relatives.'

Ashley, rather horrified by this unhappy catalogue of wifely suffering, said, 'I collect these must be neighbours.'

Caro nodded.

'Not all men are monsters. Nor are they always to blame for the troubles in a marriage,' he said, feeling compelled to defend his sex.

Her little chin tilted defiantly. 'The only marriage that I would consider is one like Lady Fraser's, whose husband leaves her here in peace while he resides in London with his mistress.'

'Surely you are jesting,' Ashley protested.

'I am not,' she replied emphatically. 'Are you married?'

'No.'

'Why not?'

Her blunt question so took him by surprise that he was betrayed into retorting, 'I have known no lady as complaisant as you.'

The big grey eyes were innocently uncomprehending. 'What do you mean?'

He had no intention of telling her and said hastily, 'Only that you are a most unusual chi—young lady.'

'I rather think I must be,' she said thoughtfully. 'My cousins, Grace and Jane, talk of nothing but clothes and catching a husband with an impressive title and fortune. They fawn over Lord Sanley, even though Mercer Corte is far handsomer, and nicer, too.'

'And does not pinch maids either.'

'No, he does not! He is in love with Emily Picton, and she with him. I cannot imagine how anyone could be in love with Lord Sanley. He is so languid and puffed-up and humorless. He expects others to entertain him while making no effort of his own.'

Yes, Ashley thought, this naïve innocent had read Sanley's character to a nicety. 'Have your cousins set their cap for Sanley?' he asked hopefully. If that were the case, they might leave him alone.

'Oh, no, he is only their second choice, but one of them will have to settle for him because they both want to rivet the same man. To hear them tell it, he is the most dashing, divinely handsome man in all England.' Caro's eyes sparkled mischievously, and Ashley was again struck by what a taking creature she could be at such moments. 'I think it shall be excessively diverting to see which of them wins him. My wager is on Grace, for she is the beauty of the family. I own that I have a lively curiosity to see a man who so impresses my cousins, for they are excessively critical of everyone else. However, Mary Milbank disapproves of him because she says that he is well known to have rakish tendencies.'

'How shocking,' Ashley exclaimed with a commendably straight face. 'Surely that must concern your cousins?'

'Not at all. They say they prefer a man who makes love charmingly. For myself, I cannot imagine anything so repulsive as being kissed by him or any man. Can you?'

'I confess that I should not like it at all,' Ashley replied with a smile, 'but I think my aversion is more understandable than yours.'

They were almost to Bellhaven's great portico now, and Ashley slowed his chestnuts to the most sedate of walks in an attempt to prolong his diverting conversation with Caro. 'Who is this repulsive gentleman that you could not imagine kissing?'

'Viscount Vinson.'

The Viscount burst out laughing as he thought of the rather numerous ladies who had welcomed his repulsive kisses.

'Why are you laughing? Do you know him?'

'Very well. I fear I am he.'

Caro was rendered speechless for what Ashley suspected might have been the first time in her life.

Finally she protested, 'But you said that your name was Ashley Neel.'

'And so it is, just as your papa is George Kelsie as well as the Marquess of Levisham.'

'But you told me that you were my father's solicitor!'

'No, you assumed that I was, as I assumed that you were a servant. So now we are even, Lady Caro,' he retorted with his most winning smile.

'What a nice smile you have,' she said approvingly. 'My cousins will be excessively happy to see you. They have been in a fit of the sullens since Mercer Corte told them that he did not think you would come on account of your hating matchmaking parties.' She examined him with frank curiosity in her eyes. 'Is it true that you are more faithful to your mistress than most men are to their wives?'

'What?' Ashley demanded incredulously.

'That is what Emily Picton told Mary Milbank when she said that you had rakish tendencies. Are you?'

Ashley, dismayed that his private affairs were apparently a matter of public discussion, said sharply, 'That is not a question a young lady of...'

'Yes, I know,' Caro interrupted impatiently, 'but I am not a lady.'

'I, however, am a gentleman, and I do not discuss such subjects with innocents,' he said firmly. Had any other woman asked him such a question he would have given her a crushing setdown, but Caro's naïve candour and innocence defused his anger.

She regarded him thoughtfully. 'Well, I dare say that if you cannot be faithful to your wife, it is laudable to be so to your mistress.'

'I do not have a wife to be faithful to,' Ashley pointed out, much nettled for a man widely reputed to have rakish tendencies.

CHAPTER FOUR

Mrs Olive Kelsie, tall and stout with a habitually discontented face, looked into Bellhaven's morning-room. The four young ladies gathered there were all dressed in the first stare of fashion, but Mrs Kelsie noted with satisfaction that her nineteen-year-old daughter Grace obscured the others with her loveliness.

Grace was statuesque, with flirtatious eyes of corn-flower blue and skin as pale and smooth as the finest ivory. Charming ringlets of guinea-gold hair framed her heart-shaped face. She was, as always, perfectly groomed in a new lavender muslin gown with not a single hair out of place.

Jane Kelsie, younger than Grace by a year, was a rather pallid copy of her elder sister, lacking her perfection of face and form but still lovely and as impeccably turned out.

Olive Kelsie was well pleased with her daughters. Grace was an Incomparable, and Jane as lovely as Emily Picton, who was such a hit in London. Mrs Kelsie, who wanted no young lady about whose charms could compete with her daughters, had tried to prevent Emily being invited, but Caroline had insisted. Mrs Kelsie had ached to strangle her niece, a longing that she felt frequently.

Thankfully, the lovely Emily had a *tendre* for Mercer Corte, Lord Corte's second son. As soon as Mrs Kelsie learned that Emily would be coming, she had seen to it that young Corte was invited, too, knowing that Emily would notice no one else. Certainly she was welcome to Corte. Although he was of a fine family, his lack of title and his modest expectations rendered him unacceptable as a possible candidate for the hand of Grace or Jane.

At the top of Olive Kelsie's list of marital prospects—and both her daughters' as well—was Lord Vinson, and she was determined that one of her girls should capture him. What a feather it would be in her cap to have her daughter—she did not much care which one—snag such a prime catch. Second on her list was Lord Sanley, the Duke of Upton's heir. Mrs Kelsie smiled to herself. She would be the talk of London if she managed to marry her daughters to a future Duke and a future Earl, especially when they were the biggest fish to be had in the marriage pond.

Continuing down the hall past the morning-room, she was well pleased at how, on the pretext that it would help his daughter, she had managed to convince her odiously disobliging brother-in-law to invite the cream of eligible males to Bellhaven. Mrs Kelsie blamed Levisham for her daughters' disappointing first season in London. Had her darlings had the proper address and clothes, they would have taken London by as great a storm as the famous Gunning sisters had done three score years earlier. But their uncle had not opened his elegant London residence for their use. Instead, they had had to rent a house with an inferior address. And he had given them only a paltry few hundred pounds for clothes instead of the several thousand that their beauty deserved. (Although Mrs Kelsie had a quite comfortable income of her own, she did not see why she should be expected to spend it on her daughters' gowns when she considered that expense the responsibility of the head of the family.)

Small wonder, given these handicaps, that Grace had received only two offers, neither of which met with her or her mama's approval, and Jane had had none. What a brilliant season they would have had if only they, not that wretched Caroline, were a Marquess's rich daughters.

Mrs Kelsie had never forgiven her late husband for dying before his brother and thereby preventing her from becoming the Marchioness of Levisham. Her only consolation lay in knowing that now her son, Tilford, would become Marquess. Poor Tilford's prospects in life had been dim until the death of Brandon, Levisham's only son, had made Tilford his uncle's heir.

Providence, which had given the ambitious Mrs Kelsie much to work with in her daughters, had been less generous in her son. No taller than his sisters, he was a plump, dour man of four and twenty, much addicted to the bottle. His lack of stature and good looks was not offset by intellectual acuity or charm, for he had neither. He was the sort of son only a mother could love, and the widow Kelsie, oblivious of his faults, doted on him.

A door behind Mrs Kelsie opened, and she turned to see her brother-in-law dressed in riding-coat and breeches. Once Levisham had been a robust man with a strong, squarish face and lively, penetrating grey eyes that bespoke keen intelligence. Now, however, his face was thin, grey and sunken, the eyes dull and listless. His clothes hung loosely, betraying the weight he had recently lost. Where once he had moved and acted quickly, with decisive energy, now he did so slowly, as though the effort were almost too much for him.

His decline had begun last spring when he had been stricken with a fever that had very nearly killed him. Although he had survived, it could not be said that he had truly recovered. His body remained frail and tired, regaining neither the weight nor the energy that the fever had sucked from him.

'Come with me to the estate-room,' he told his sister-in-law. 'I wish to discuss Tilford with you.'

Mrs Kelsie bit her lip angrily. For some inexplicable reason, the Marquess held her darling Tilford in particular repugnance. This antipathy was a daunting—and exceedingly vexing—impediment to her most cherished scheme: to marry her son to Caroline.

Not that Mrs Kelsie approved of having that ramshackle girl for a daughter-in-law. It was shocking the way Levisham had let her run wild: riding bareback, climbing trees, and even, if one particularly horrifying report was to be credited, swimming half naked in her shift. But although Caroline was unattractive to her aunt, the great fortune that the chit had inherited from her mother was irresistible. Only the Bellhaven estate, which would be frightfully expensive to keep up, and the house in London were entailed. The rest of Levisham's fortune was his to do with as he wished, and he would leave it to Caroline, who did not need a sixpence of it, instead of to her poor Tilford.

If her son—and she with him—were to live in the style his title required, he would have to marry a fortune. Much as she doted on him, even she had to admit that he did not acquit himself well in society. With so many odiously handsome fortune-hunters stalking even ugly heiresses of sizeable fortunes, his chances of claiming one as his wife were not high. Olive, who had been in charge of Levisham's guest list, had invited Mary Milbank, an heiress to a considerable fortune, but the bran-faced creature had been so rude as to make clear her contempt for Tilford last night. Caroline remained Tilford's best hope of marrying an heiress. Besides, he had developed a quite unaccountable *tendre* for his skinny little cousin.

The Marquess led his sister-in-law into a small room dominated by a massive carved mahogany desk that had been designed for his great-grandfather by William Kent. Along one wall, a mahogany bookcase held an impressive number of account-books, all neatly labelled. On the wall facing his desk hung a large painting of the late Marchioness, a delicate beauty with a halo of golden curls. At first glance, she looked like an ethereal angel until one noticed the mischievous expression in her big sea-blue eyes.

As Levisham closed the door, Mrs Kelsie noted how weary and frail he looked. It would not be long before her darling Tilford would be the Marquess and Caroline his ward. Then Olive would impose on her niece the strict discipline that she needed. A few whippings would do her a world of good. And no one could stop Tilford from marrying her. Once she was his ward, then his wife, life would be very different indeed for the annoying brat.

The Marquess gestured with a thin hand for Mrs Kelsie to sit in an uncomfortable straight-backed chair. No doubt he was going to cut up stiff over poor Tilford's having become a trifle bosky at dinner last night, and she tried to divert him by asking, 'Do you approve of the guests that I invited?'

'But of course. I knew that you could be depended upon to select the best male catches on the marriage mart without a fortune-hunter among them.'

Discomfited by the mockery in his voice that she did not understand, she said stiffly, 'I felt it my duty to see that dearest Caroline was introduced to the most eligible of possible suitors.'

'Did you, indeed?' The Marquess lifted an eyebrow. '*Dearest* Caroline will not thank you. You know that she is passionately opposed to marrying.'

For which Mrs Kelsie was most grateful. Levisham would never force Caroline to do anything, so she would remain single until after her father's death, when Tilford could claim her. Her aunt, concealing her delight at this situation, exclaimed, 'Surely you cannot want dearest Caroline to be an ape-leader?'

'Of course not,' Levisham admitted.

'Nor I. That is why I have taken such care to invite the most eligible young bachelors. Perhaps one of them will fall in love with her and make her forget her objections,' Olive lied. None of the male guests, who could have the pick of the marriage mart, would be attracted by such a thin slip of a girl with a brown complexion, unruly hair, and a wretched tongue that had already given both Sanley and Sir Percival a disgust of her. Nevertheless, Olive had taken the further precaution of isolating Caro between herself and her son at meals. If Olive had thought that one of the male guests might take a fancy to Caroline, she would never have suggested the party. Great as her ambitions were for her daughters, her darling Tilford took precedence.

Levisham said thoughtfully, 'Despite their outrageous cost, I do not think the clothes you convinced me Caro must have suit her well.'

Olive felt something akin to fear prickle at her. Surely he could not suspect that she had worked out a special arrangement with her dressmaker. The amount of fabric ordered for each of her niece's gowns had been enough for Grace or Jane to have one, too, and the cost of making it up had been concealed in the price charged for Caroline's. The Marquess unknowingly had paid for two dresses for each one that his daughter had got. Furthermore, Olive had seen to it that Caroline's gowns enhanced her numerous bad features.

'It is not the clothes,' Olive said, hiding her unease in vehemence, 'but the careless way dearest Caroline wears them. She runs about like a scullery-maid with her hems crooked, her ruffles torn and her hair falling down.'

At that moment, the young lady herself scampered by the estate-room window in a faded blue calico frock, and her aunt was able to say, 'Only look at her now. All the beautiful gowns I had made for her, and what is she wearing but a wretched dress that is years old.'

Levisham frowned. 'When we are finished here, tell Caro that I wish to see her.'

'I'll do so immediately,' Olive said, rising from her chair in the hope of escaping before her brother-in-law recalled the reason he wished to speak with her.

'No, not until we discuss Tilford's disgusting behaviour last night, treating us to that tasteless, drunken harangue and then passing out in a stupor in the drawing-room. To ensure that there is no repeat of this, I have ordered that the servants pour him no wine tonight. He is to drink nothing for the remainder of his stay here. I will not have him disgrace us again.'

Olive was outraged that he could talk of her darling Tilford so after the way his own rag-mannered daughter had mortified them with her incorrigible tongue and behaviour. Neither Lord Sanley nor Sir Percival would ever forgive her. Worse, Jane had seen her sneaking out early that morning to ride bareback, even though her aunt had prohibited her from doing so while guests were at Bellhaven. 'Tilford was only slightly in the altitudes, and it was nothing compared to what dearest Car—'

The Marquess cut Olive off. 'Tilford was drunk as a wheelbarrow. If he does not abide by my orders, he will leave Bellhaven on the morrow.'

Olive recognised from the implacability of Levisham's tone that it would do no good to argue with him. How infuriating that she had never been able to bring him under her thumb as she had both his brother and her son, who would never have dared to oppose her in anything. She cried petulantly, 'I do not know how you can be so hard on poor Tilford when Caroline flagrantly disobeys me.'

'What has she done?'

'Sneaked out to ride bareback this morning. What will our guests think of such shameless conduct?'

'I doubt that any of them will be up early enough to witness it,' Levisham replied calmly.

This indulgent answer further fuelled Mrs Kelsie's rage. If Levisham would not require Caroline to obey her, she would find another way to enforce her edicts. She was not a woman to be defied. By heaven above, she would do whatever was necessary to impose her will upon that disgraceful hoyden.

CHAPTER FIVE

WHEN CARO entered the estate-room in answer to her father's summons, he was standing by the corner of his big desk, looking sadly preoccupied, and his eyes did not light up as they usually did when he saw her. She had seen that unhappy look frequently recently, but when she asked him what was wrong, he would deny that anything was. Seeking to divert his thoughts to more cheerful channels, she said, 'Oh, Papa, I have just seen the most splendid pair of chestnuts. You would be proud to own them.'

'Where did you see them?'

'They belong to Lord Vinson. He gave me a ride behind them. He is a top sawyer with the ribbons, and so nice, too. I like him the best of all our guests.'

The Marquess asked anxiously, 'Did you meet Vinson looking as you do now?'

Caro glanced down at her faded, paw-stained dress, then back up at her father in surprise. Unlike her Aunt Olive, who raised such dust-ups about how she acted and dressed, Papa never seemed to mind.

But now he said in a reproving tone that he had never before used with her, 'Look at you! That dress should have been consigned to the rag-bag and your skirt is covered with dirty prints.'

This censure, coming from her beloved father, who never criticised her, stung Caro as painfully as a whiplash. She hung her head, acutely aware of how untidy she looked.

'No doubt you gave Lord Vinson a disgust of you, looking the way you do,' Levisham said, frowning unhappily.

Remembering how shocked Vinson had been when he had learned her identity, Caro knew that her father was right. This realisation was oddly painful to her. Ashley was so understanding and so much fun to talk to. And so very handsome, too. She could see now why her cousins were wildly infatuated with him. He was not at all toplofty like Lord Sanley or affected like Sir Percival. So different, too, from her dour cousin Tilford. A shudder of revulsion coursed through Caro at the thought of him.

'Your aunt has been complaining to me about your appearance, Caro, and she is quite right to do so.'

Caro bit her lip. Her appearance was not, as her aunt seemed to think, deliberate. She would have liked nothing better than to be as immaculately turned out as Grace and Jane, but no matter how hard she tried, she could never manage to look neat and stylish and cool as her cousins did.

Her hair, fine as silk and unruly as a colt, defied all attempts to confine it in a neat coil or knot. Long skirts, too, were a severe trial. Her hems never seemed to hang quite straight, perhaps because she frequently hitched up her skirts to climb fences that got in her way. For some maddening reason, her ruffles seemed especially prone to catch and tear. She could rarely remember to slow her purposeful, impatient gait to the sedate, graceful glide of a lady. Nor could she hide her boisterous high spirits and irrepressible candour behind the colourless decorum that her aunt insisted was the mark of a young lady of quality.

'How do you expect to attract a husband, looking as you do?' her father demanded in exasperation.

Caro's head snapped up. 'But, Papa, you know that I do not intend to marry. I shall devote myself to you as Abigail Foster did to her father.' Abigail, a pretty woman of wit and intelligence a decade older than Caro, had rejected several flattering offers, refusing to surrender herself to a husband's domination. Instead she had dedicated herself to caring for her widowed father, an old curmudgeon whom Caro secretly had not thought worthy of Abigail's devotion.

Levisham's frown deepened at the mention of Abigail. 'I think that both you and she were too much affected by Lady Fraser's jaundiced views of marriage. Remember that Lady Fraser and her husband disliked each other from the moment they met. Their parents were fools to have forced them into an arranged marriage. Never were two people more ill suited. He cares only for London and its parties; she, for the country and her horses. And both have suffered.'

It was true that Caro's views of marriage, and of Lord Fraser, too, had been darkly coloured by his lady, and she cried angrily, 'I never thought to hear you defend that odious man.'

'To Lord Fraser's credit, he permits her to live where she wishes with their son, although he would prefer the boy to be with him in London.'

'Will you also make excuses for Potter and Burk and Coleberd?' Caro cried. Her kind heart, which could not bear suffering of any nature, grieved for their poor, mistreated wives.

'No, I do not. While I grant you that Lady Fraser can cite unfortunate examples, such as those, of ill-treated wives, there are also a great many happy ones,' Levisham said. 'Furthermore, look at how unhappy Abigail Foster is now that her father is dead. She would have been wiser to have accepted . . . one of the offers she rejected.'

Caro, whose soft heart ached for poor Abigail, had a difficult time fighting back tears. Upon the death of Abigail's father eight months ago, his country seat had passed to his son and heir. The latter's shrewish wife, determined not to share the house with the woman who had so long presided over it, had not rested until Abigail was packed off against her will to live with a crotchety old aunt in Glasgow.

'I beg of you to consider carefully, Caro, whether marriage would not have been preferable for Abigail to her present situation.'

'But I do not have an odious sister-in-law,' Caro objected.

'You may have worse,' he said abruptly.

'Papa, what are you talking about? Surely you cannot want me to marry,' Caro protested in a small, betrayed voice. 'You have always said that you wished me to remain with you.'

Her father, looking quite as miserable as she felt, said sharply, 'Like Abigail's father, I shall not live forever. Furthermore, I want grandchildren. With Brandon dead, you are my only chance for them. I beg of you to reconsider your opposition to marriage. You could find among our guests one who would make you a good, loving husband.'

'I do not want a loving husband,' Caro cried passionately. 'I find the thought of such attentions repugnant.'

Clearly startled by her vehemence, Levisham said softly, 'But, my child, that is only because you have not yet met a man who has touched your heart.'

'And I never shall,' she cried impetuously. 'If I must marry, I pray that it be a marriage like Lady Fraser's.'

'You cannot mean that, Caro. They never see each other, and he lives with another.'

'I mean it most sincerely. It is precisely the kind of marriage that I want. I cannot bear the thought of a man touching me.'

Her father looked thoroughly alarmed. 'What has given you such an excessive aversion to men?'

Caro longed to tell him, but she had given her solemn word to Tilford that she would not, and she could never go back on that. A month before, while her father had been away on a two-day inspection of another of his estates, Tilford had appeared, thoroughly foxed, at Bellhaven. Caro had been in the deserted stables inspecting a new foal, and he had trapped her there.

Before she had realised what he was about, he had crushed her to him, his odorous breath nauseating her. Then his mouth had ground down on hers with such force that her lip had bled.

For Caro, who had never before been kissed, it had confirmed her worst apprehensions about men and marriage. So this was what a man's lovemaking was like, she had thought with revulsion. In that brief, brutal encounter, Tilford had sealed her determination never to marry and subject herself to a husband's cruel, repugnant desires.

She had kicked and scratched and struggled until she had escaped his embrace. When he had started after her, she had picked up a bucket of water and thrown it over him. It had brought him to his senses, and he had begged her forgiveness.

She had told him bluntly what she thought of him.

To her amazement, he had begun to cry, begging her, with tears streaming down his cheeks, not to tell either his mother or her father. Caro, who had always before felt more pity than dislike for her oafish, slow-topped cousin, was incapable of resisting anyone's tears, and she had given him her word that she would not tell. After all, informing her father, who hated having Tilford as his heir, would only make the Marquess more unhappy.

'I repeat, Caro,' her father was saying in alarm, 'what has given you such an abhorrence of men?'

Unable to tell him the truth, she cried, 'I have only to look about me! I will never marry!'

CHAPTER SIX

DINNER that night proved to be far livelier than it had been on the previous evening, thanks to the addition of Lord Vinson to the company. He frequently kept those around him in laughter, but Caro, seated at the opposite end of the table between her aunt and Tilford, could catch only occasional snatches of what Ashley said, and she found herself straining her ears vainly to hear more.

Vinson was flanked by Grace and Jane. On the other side of Grace was Lord Sanley, the Duke of Upton's son. Jane had drawn Lord Charles Harley, the Earl of Wendover's heir. Caro, who had been been uneasy with Tilford since the incident in the stables, had wanted to cry with vexation when she had discovered that she was again seated between him and her aunt, who was presiding at the foot of the table.

Sitting next to Tilford robbed her of whatever appetite she might have had. Her only consolation was that tonight he was not getting foxed, which always made him argumentative and loudly obnoxious. His wine-glass remained empty, and the servant stationed behind him made no attempt to fill it. Once Tilford touched it as if to call the minion's attention to it, but his hand dropped away hastily at a quelling look from his mother. He remained sullen and silent as a stone throughout the meal.

After dinner, the men stayed behind in the dining-room to enjoy coffee and brandy with their host while

Aunt Olive led the females into the drawing-room. Although it was large and formal, its walls hung with Spitalfields silk brocade and the ceiling with three crystal chandeliers, it had a comfortable, inviting atmosphere that was achieved by the invitingly casual groupings of settees and armchairs.

Caro and Emily listened quietly as Grace, Jane, their mother and Mary Milbank cruelly dissected the absent males. Lord Charles Harley was the most cruelly maligned. His nickname was the Nose, and even Caro had to concede that his face did appear to be all proboscis. Worse, its enormous size had the misfortune to project from an excessively sloping forehead and receding chin that gave him a startling triangular profile. But Caro liked him. He was intelligent, friendly and good-hearted, all qualities she valued far more than a nose.

But clearly Jane did not. With one hand pulling on her nose to extend its length, she acted out a cruelly slanderous lampoon of poor Lord Charles. Her mother, sister and Mary Milbank laughed uproariously, while Emily and Caro sat in uncomfortable silence.

Only Ashley escaped criticism. Even Mary seemed to have either forgiven or forgotten his rakish tendencies as she joined the Kelsie daughters in complimenting his charm, fine looks, impeccable dress, good manners and wit.

Grace turned suddenly to Caro, who had taken no part in the conversation. 'Which of our guests would you like to marry?'

Caro, taken aback by the abruptness of the question, answered, 'None of them. You know that I wish never to marry.'

'You say that because you know only a fortune-hunter would marry an antidote like you,' Grace scoffed.

Caro's pride would not allow her cousins the satisfaction of knowing how much their many cruel jibes hurt her. She either pretended to take no notice or shrugged them off with a cool comment as though they mattered naught. Caro displayed the same feigned indifference to their mother's incessant criticism. Now, forcing a smile to her lips, she said, 'I say it because I am not so foolish as to think marriage need be a woman's only purpose in life.'

But part of her opposition to marriage stemmed from the knowledge that no man would ever fall madly in love with a plain thing like herself. Were she to receive an offer, it would be, as Grace said, based on other considerations, principally her fortune. Caro had observed the unhappy fate of plain heiresses, such as Amelia Colebard and Clara Potter, and she had no intention of sharing it. She had seen no example of a husband who, having married for other than love, treated his wife well.

When the men rejoined the ladies in the drawing-room after finishing their brandy, most of them gravitated immediately towards Grace and Jane, who, in complementary shades of pink and blue, were artfully arranged on a sofa with their mama beside them.

Mercer Corte and Vinson, coming into the drawing-room together, went immediately towards Emily Picton, but Mrs Kelsie insisted that Ashley join her and her daughters on the sofa. As he crossed to it, Caro wondered in mortification how she could ever have mistaken him for a solicitor. The quiet elegance of his faultlessly tailored midnight-blue coat and white breeches, and the intricate arrangement of his snowy cravat with a single sapphire glittering in its folds, eclipsed his far more showily dressed companions, even that satin-clad pink of the ton, Sir Percival Plymtree, whose waistcoat was crowded with fobs and seals as his fingers were with rings.

Caro was suddenly conscious of how deficient her own appearance was and wished that she had spent more time on her toilette. She was wearing one of the new gowns that Aunt Olive had ordered for her, a skimpily cut blue muslin. Although her aunt had proclaimed it perfect on her, it seemed to Caro to emphasise her thin, boyish form, and its colour did not become her complexion at all.

Lord Charles joined Caro, who, remembering how Jane had made fun of his nose, went out of her way to be friendly with him. A few minutes later, Ashley left the sofa and the Kelsie sisters to join Mercer and Emily. Jane, accompanied by Mary Milbank, promptly came up to Charles and Caro.

It was not long before Jane had the audacity to compliment poor Charles's nose, saying it gave him a noble appearance.

'Do you truly think so?' he asked eagerly.

'Oh, yes,' Jane cooed.

Incensed by such duplicity, Caro detached herself from the group and moved away. Having never before been exposed to the *haut monde* or the mating game of its young, she was repelled by the machinations of the females as they homed in on male targets, even those they professed not to like. Hypocrisy shocked her, and she could not fathom how they could simper so sweetly to a gentleman after savaging him behind his back.

'What has inspired such a furious look, Lady Caro?' enquired Ashley's voice behind her.

An odd little tremor of pleasure that he had sought her out coursed through her, and she turned to him with a smile. He was so tall and she so small that the top of her head did not reach his shoulder. Incurably honest as always, she told him of her cousin's mendacity, adding passionately, 'I would not object to her making fun of Sir Percival's corset or of Paul Coleman's front teeth, which he's so foolishly filed into points. But I think it is excessively cruel and unjust to ridicule an unfortunate nose that one cannot help. Then to toad-eat him to his face is the outside of enough!'

She looked at Ashley defiantly, half expecting him to tell her she was a silly goose, but he merely said gravely, 'I quite agree.' He smiled at her, saying lightly, 'I imagine all us poor males suffered from Jane's fault-finding tongue.'

'Oh, not you!' Caro exclaimed. 'Even Mary Milbank seems to have forgotten your rakish tendencies. I dare say that between her and my cousins you shall not have a moment's peace.'

He frowned at her words, but before she could ask him what was wrong, Aunt Olive and her daughters bore down upon them like a flagship flanked by two frigates.

'Dear Lord Vinson,' Aunt Olive began, 'I do hope that dearest Caroline has not shocked or insulted you. She has the most wayward tongue. One never knows what will pop out of her mouth.'

'To the contrary, I find her conversation charming.'

'How gallant you are,' Aunt Olive twittered, coyly fluttering her fan. 'Caroline dearest, do repair your hair. It is flying all about. And I do believe you have spilled something on your new gown, too. What a clumsy child you are. You have surely given Lord Vinson a disgust of you, although he is too polite to say anything.'

Caro, ready to sink at being chastised so in front of Ashley, turned away.

As she fled, Aunt Olive said in long-suffering accents, 'I have tried so diligently to make dearest Caroline into a lady, but I fear the task is hopeless, Lord Vinson. She serves to remind me, however, how fortunate I am in my own two daughters who, I do believe, were born perfect young ladies, so superior have their behaviour and manners always been.'

Caro, humiliated by her aunt's words, stopped in front of a mirror in the hall to examine her gown. She could find no trace of the spot her aunt had talked about.

After the ladies and most of the gentlemen had retired to their rooms that night, Ashley opened one of the French doors that led from the drawing-room to the terrace, and slipped outside. The night had been very still and hot, but a cooling breeze was at last wafting across the terrace that ran the length of Bellhaven's elegant south front.

Seating himself on the stone balustrade that overlooked the formal garden, he considered with cynical amusement the guests who had been invited to Bellhaven. With the exception of Mercer Corte, the males were all bachelors of great fortune and impressive family. Some of them, like buffle-headed Paul Coleman or that malicious gossip, Percy Plymtree, had nothing else to recommend them. Which convinced Ashley that they must have been chosen by that scheming Olive Kelsie. When she had accused her niece of disgusting him, it had been all he could do to keep from telling the harridan that it was she, not her niece, who did so.

Although Caro did not disgust him, she had sorely disappointed him. On the road to Bellhaven, his one sustaining hope had been that she would be a diamond of the first water whom he would come to love.

But she had turned out to be a child, an amusing one to be sure, but a child none the less. And one shockingly wanting in conduct at that. Yet he would have much preferred to have been seated beside her at dinner instead of between her two far lovelier cousins.

That meal had been Ashley's longest continuous exposure to Grace and Jane Kelsie. By the time the ladies had risen from the table to leave the men to their coffee and brandy, he had realised with dismaying clarity what dead bores they both were. Furthermore, he was now certain that beneath their gushing exterior, as syrupy as sugar-water, they were very much like their domineering shrew of a mother.

He thought glumly of the other girls on his father's list: Emily Picton was in love with Mercer Corte; Lady Margaret was beautiful but boring and stupid; Elizabeth Trott's self-absorption offended him; Mary Milbank was dull and missish in the bargain; and Caro was too young.

Hearing footsteps, Ashley looked up to see Mercer Corte approaching him.

'Such a beastly hot night,' Mercer said, settling beside Ashley on the stone balustrade. He lowered his voice to a whisper. 'I'm devilish glad you came. I happened on something very early on the day I left London for here that greatly disturbed me. I saw again the one-eared man who was lurking in Curzon Street before your brother's race.'

'Where?' Ashley asked eagerly.

'In the back slums of St Giles, with your cousin Henry.'

'Good lord!' Ashley exclaimed. 'What the devil were you doing in such a wretched spot?'

'Paul Coleman dragged me there. Insisted he wanted to explore the Holy Land, and he was so in his cups that I did not dare leave him to do so on his own.' Mercer shuddered visibly. 'Why it's called the Holy Land is beyond me. I have never seen such squalor and degradation and misery in my life.'

'Horrifying, isn't it,' Ashley said grimly. ' 'Tis said to get its name because its residents are more holey in their garments than righteous in their conduct.'

'That's true enough! Never felt so uncomfortable in my life as I did in that boozing-ken where I saw your cousin. I don't mind admitting that I felt lucky to get out of there without my throat being slit. Your cousin was huddled in a secluded corner with the one-eared man.'

Ashley jumped up from the balustrade, much agitated, and began pacing in front of Mercer. 'Are you absolutely certain that it was the same man that you saw coming from the stable that night?'

Mercer, looking up at Ashley as he towered above him, met his gaze steadily. 'No doubt about it. If you ever saw him, you would not mistake another for him. He's a hulking bruiser, as ugly as mud, with two nasty scars on his face. And, of course, his right ear is missing. As soon as I saw your cousin with him, I thought about those horrifying rumors about Henry and that fatal race.'

Ashley's hands unconsciously clenched into angry fists. He had thought that Henry, whatever his other faults might be, was not a murderer. But in the face of this new evidence, his father's suspicions appeared to be nearer to the truth. But why would his cousin have wanted to kill William? Surely it had not been merely to win a large sum on the curricle race? Henry did not need the blunt, having been very plump in the pockets since he had won a hundred thousand pounds from Lord Whittleson two years ago in one sitting.

There could be only one possible motive for Henry to kill William, and it chilled Ashley to the marrow. His cousin must mean to inherit the Bourn title and fortune. But before he could do that, he would also have to eliminate two additional obstacles in his path: the Earl and Ashley. If Henry was cold-blooded enough to have murdered William, he would not hesitate to kill again. Ashley had to find out the truth, if not from Henry, then from the one-eared man.

The Viscount sat down again on the balustrade beside Mercer. 'When we get back to London, would you take me to that alehouse?'

Mercer nodded reluctantly. 'Yes, although I would prefer never to see it or St Giles again.'

For a few moments they sat in silence broken only by the cry of a night bird.

At length, Mercer said, 'I confess that I am surprised you came to Bellhaven. Clearly it is a matchmaking party for Levisham's nieces, and such affairs were never your cup of tea.'

'Nor are they now,' Ashley confessed, staring moodily at the long row of French doors that lined the terrace. Several of them had been opened in an attempt to cool the dark rooms behind them. 'I am only here at my father's dictate. He has decided that it is time for me to marry and produce an heir.'

Mercer grinned at him. 'And what do you say to that, or do I dare ask?'

'He is right,' Ashley said glumly. 'That is why I am here.'

Mercer's smile faded. 'Are you hoaxing me? I thought that you had eyes for no woman but Lady Roxley.'

'I don't. But since she is already married, I can hardly wed her.'

'I collect that you have a lady in mind.'

'*I* do not, but my father has seven from which I may choose. Five of them, including your charming Emily, are here, so now you understand why I am, too.'

'Are you telling me you mean to try to fix your interest with Emily?' Mercer cried, firing up.

'Good God, no! You are my friend. I would not try to do so even if I thought it were possible, which it clearly is not. She adores you.'

'Not as much as I adore her.'

'How very lucky you are,' Ashley said, sighing. 'I had always thought that when I married it would be for love. Fate has decreed otherwise. So now I may choose from the Kelsie sisters, Mary Milbank or Lady Caro.'

'But Caro is a mere child,' Mercer protested.

'Utterly unsuitable,' Ashley agreed, 'but my father was unaware of that. It had been reported to him that she favoured her mother.'

'Which, of course, she does not. I've seen the Marchioness's portrait. What a beauty she was! Poor Caro is so plain, although I confess I find her delightful. I wager that Sanley never had such a setdown in his life as she gave him yesterday.'

'I am sorry that I missed it.'

'You should be,' Mercer assured him with a grin. 'My Emily is much attached to Caro. She says that there is no more honest, generous and kind-hearted girl alive than Caro, even though she sometimes says and does outrageous things. Which one of the fair ladies on your father's list do you mean to choose as your bride?'

'As long as I cannot wed a woman I love, it matters naught to me which one I marry!'

'Now you are hoaxing me,' Mercer protested. 'Surely you must have some criteria.'

Ashley's lips curled in a bitter little smile. 'Only that she be a woman of exceptional understanding.'

Mercer nodded his head in comprehension. 'In other words, one who will understand about Estelle.'

'How astute you are, Merce.'

'I suspect a number of women would be willing to overlook Lady Roxley in exchange for the opportunity to become Countess of Bourn.'

'At least until the knot is tied,' Ashley retorted cynically. 'The difficulty is in finding a lady whose superior understanding will last beyond our wedding vows. If I find her, she is the one I shall marry.'

A stout figure in a satin wrapper drew back from one of the second-storey windows overlooking the terrace where Ashley and Mercer were talking. Olive Kelsie was well pleased with the fruit of her eavesdropping.

So Vinson was ripe for the plucking. All that would be required to shackle him was to convince him of how broad-minded her daughters were. Now the only remaining difficulty was which of them should have him. Both were infatuated with him, but their mother favoured Jane for the very practical reason that Grace would have the better chance of snaring Lord Sanley.

Downstairs from Mrs Kelsie, a second eavesdropper, as edified as the first, stepped back from the shadows of a French door that was slightly open, fading deeper into the darkness that had concealed him from the two men on the balustrade, and began laying very different plans.

CHAPTER SEVEN

THE ROOM was grey with the first light of dawn when Ashley awoke the following morning, sorely troubled by the marital commitment that he must make. Despite his careless words to Mercer Corte that it mattered not at all which of the young ladies on his father's list he married, he did not, in truth, want to marry any of them.

What he needed, he decided, was a bruising ride to lift his spirits. But he could hardly invade his host's stables at this early hour without his permission, so he decided to settle for a walk in Bellhaven's park instead. Fortunately, he was not a man dependent on his valet. When he had finished his morning ablutions, donned his double-breasted brown riding-coat and buckskin breeches, and tied his white linen neckcloth with a skill that would have left Brummel envious, Ashley looked so well turned out that any valet would have been proud to take credit for having dressed him.

Ashley's room faced east, and he stopped at the window to enjoy the beauty of the sunrise that streaked the sky. His peripheral vision caught a dash of red fluttering to the ground from another window further down the wall. Startled, he stared down at what appeared to be a girl's skirt lying on the ground beneath a large, gracious elm. Foreboding seized him as his eyes travelled up the tree.

He was not entirely surprised, though none the less horrified, to see Caro inching her way along one of the elm's sturdy limbs. Her position, combined with the riding-breeches she wore, gave him a tantalising view of her little derrière. Good lord, the chit would break her neck yet! He dared not call out to her, for fear he would startle her as he had yesterday and she would fall.

He dashed out of his room and down a back staircase that he had noticed the previous night. But when he came out in the rustic, his progress was checked as he blundered about its dreary, unfamiliar halls looking for an exit. Finally he found one, but it brought him out behind the steps of the portico, and he had to run round to the east side of the building.

As he turned the corner, he was vastly relieved to see that Caro was not lying crumpled at the foot of the elm. But his relief quickly faded as he realised that both she and her skirt had disappeared.

Hearing a horse galloping from the stable, he turned towards the sound. Caro, riding bareback, her hair streaming loose in the wind, was racing away on a fleet white pony. It would do no good to call to her. She was too far away to hear him over the sound of her mount's hooves. He cursed under his breath. If she did not know the dangers attendant on such a ramshackle ride, he did.

Noting the direction in which she was headed, he ran to the stable, which was barren of human presence. Hanging from a peg in the tack-room was the long red skirt that Caro had dropped from the window. Grabbing a bridle and saddle, he selected a swift-looking mount and within five minutes was thundering down the path he had seen her take.

It was another ten minutes before he had her in sight, and then only because she had slowed her mount to a canter in a pretty lane banked by goldenrod and heather, where the air was scented with the sweet smell of bedstraw.

He galloped towards her, calling, 'Caro, stop!'

She complied. When he reached her, the guilty expression on her mischievous face reminded him of William's three-year-old daughter when Ashley had caught her clandestinely sampling a plate of little cakes prepared for her mama's guests.

'What are you doing here?' she demanded.

'Coming after you. I saw that you were again in need of rescue.'

'I was not!' she responded ungratefully.

'You cannot ride alone like this.'

'Oh, fustian! You are as tiresome as my aunt.' Her little lower lip protruded stubbornly. 'And I thought you were a prime 'un,' she said in a tone of deep disillusionment.

Ashley felt it was his unhappy duty to increase Caro's indignation by warning her that she was likely to break her neck if she persisted in leaving second-storey rooms via the window.

'Oh, no, it is not the least dangerous when there is a tree there,' she reassured him.

A dark suspicion crossed his mind. 'Have you done so when there was no tree?'

She nodded. 'When I was thirteen, my aunt prevailed upon Papa to send me to stay with her for a week. It was dreadful. Even then she was determined that I should be a lady, and she would not let me do any of the things I liked. When I sneaked out early to ride, she caught me and locked me in my room. But there was no tree.'

'How did you overcome that difficulty?'

'I tied the bedclothes together into a makeshift rope and climbed down them. It was capital fun!'

The hoyden was incorrigible! 'Was it not exceedingly difficult to return by that route?' Ashley demanded.

'I did not have to. Aunt Olive left the key in the lock, so I was able to open it from the hall and creep back in. She generally slept until noon, and never suspected that I, not one of the maids, had unlocked it.'

'But why the devil did you choose such an unorthodox route to depart from the house this morning?'

'The door to my room was locked. I am certain that it was Aunt Olive again. She has prohibited my early morning rides while guests are here.'

Ashley was shocked. 'She must have locked it because she is concerned about your safety.' Even as these words left his mouth, he was conscious that he was most likely telling a whisker. The emotion he had seen in Mrs Kelsie's eyes when she gazed upon her niece was something very different from either concern or affection.

Caro shrugged. 'Perhaps, but I think it is because she cannot bear to be disobeyed.'

Disgusted as he was by her aunt, Ashley was still conscious of his duty as an Older Person. 'Do you not think it wrong to disobey her?'

'She is not my guardian, although she orders me about as though she were. Nor did I give her my word that I would not ride,' Caro cried, as if that made all the difference. 'Had I done that, I would never have broken it.'

He could not help but be impressed by how seriously she regarded the sacredness of her word. 'Does your father know that your aunt locked you in your room?' Ashley had seen the previous night the deep love with which Levisham watched his daughter, and was certain that he would not condone her aunt's action.

'No, and I shan't tell him, for she will only deny it and will find some way to get back at me for telling Papa.' She frowned unhappily. 'It is a terrible thing to say, but I fear that my aunt is not always a truthful woman.'

Ashley suspected that this observation was as true as it was sincere. Caro's little brown face, which seemed all eyes, reminded Ashley of a wood-sprite. He wondered what he should do now. Although she was clearly oblivious of the dangers attendant upon careering bareback and alone about the countryside, he was not. Yet he knew that any request that she return with him to the house would meet with instant rejection. Instead, he asked, 'Would you give me a tour of Bellhaven's park, elfin?'

'Why do you call me that?'

He grinned. 'Because it describes you so well. Shall we ride?'

They took a circuitous route through the park, Caro showing him all the favourite spots where she and her brother Brandon had played. By the time they headed back towards the stable an hour later, Ashley had acquired, from her running comments interspersed with adroit questioning on his part, a fair notion of the isolated, protected life that she had led.

She and her brother had grown up with only each other as playmates, except when Emily had visited her grandfather, who lived on a neighbouring property.

'Since my brother died, there has been no one else to talk to when Papa is busy with the estate.' Caro's face clouded. 'I miss Brandon so. We did everything together. Do you have a brother?'

'I did, but he, too, is dead.'

'Oh, I am sorry,' she cried, reaching out to touch Ashley's arm in an instinctive gesture of comfort, her big grey eyes radiating sorrow and sympathy.

Ashley, used to far more sophisticated, scheming women, was struck—and touched—by Caro's innate, uncalculating sweetness.

'You must miss him dreadfully,' she murmured.

'I mourn for him, but I fear we were never very close. He was much older than I.' Ashley had loved his half-brother, but pompous, humourless William had had no patience with a mischievous, fun-loving little boy nine years his junior, especially one who could not learn to treat the elder brother with the deference and respect William had thought his due.

It was clear from what Caro said that her father had cut himself and his children off from not only the ton but most of his neighbours, too. Apparently finding the latter—including the drunken Mr Burk, Sir John Wesley, the wastrel, and Mr Potter, the wife-beater—brutish and boring, the Marquess had restricted his social circle to Barton Picton, Emily's paternal grandfather, the Reverend Mr Laken, who held the living, Dr Baxter, the local physician, and Sir Ronald Foster and his daughter Abigail, who had clearly been an important influence on Caro.

Ashley had known Abigail Foster, a very pretty, witty woman who would be twenty-eight now, since she was his own age. During her first season in London she had turned down several excellent offers for her hand. She had done so, Caro confided admiringly to Ashley, because she refused to give herself over to the uncertain mercy of a husband. Instead she devoted herself to her father, an example that Caro was determined to emulate. Ashley suspected that Abigail Foster had had a stronger influence on Caro's views of marriage than Lady Fraser.

By the time they returned to the stable, he had learned that Caro had never been further from Bellhaven than the local village, and that he and his fellow guests were her first exposure to the fashionable world to which she had been born.

As they reached the stable, she said, 'Promise me that you will not tell my aunt or my father about our ride. She would ring such a dreadful peal over me, and Papa will not like it either.'

'I promise I won't tell your aunt, but it is my duty to tell your father.'

'If you do, you shall be in my black books permanently,' Caro said firmly.

Ashley was saved from this dire fate, however, because her father was in the stableyard when they stopped their mounts. Giving Ashley a cold, searching look, he demanded, 'Where have you and my daughter been?'

'Don't fly into the boughs, Papa,' Caro said calmly, jumping down from her horse. 'He saw me leaving and would not permit me to ride alone. I own I do not apprehend why riding alone sinks me below reproach.'

She handed the reins of her pony to a groom and strode into the stable to collect her skirt.

Her father turned his weary, sunken face to Ashley. 'I collect that I owe you both gratitude and an apology. I had an uneasy moment.'

'Yes,' Ashley said drily, 'your daughter informs me that I have a reputation for rakish tendencies. However, I assure you that I have never trifled with innocents.'

'If you knew Caro better, you would understand my concern. She is not fly to the time of day, and she naïvely tumbles into trouble without being aware that she is in it. I tried to shelter her from all that is unpleasant in life, and in the process I fear I have let her remain a child too long. How is it that you noticed her leaving this morning?'

'Her departure was difficult to ignore. She was climbing down the tree outside her window.'

'Good God! She always was half monkey, but why the tree?'

'Her door was locked; by her aunt, she thinks.'

Levisham's face reddened in anger. 'That evil woman! Why did Caro not tell me?'

'She believes that her aunt will only deny it.'

'And Caro is right,' the Marquess said grimly. 'Olive knows I would not permit such a thing. How I wish I could send her and her drunken son packing immediately, but . . .'

'But her presence is required for propriety until your guests depart.'

Levisham nodded, then asked abruptly, 'Are you excessively shocked by my daughter's unconventional tongue and behaviour?'

Ashley was disconcerted by the speculative look that had suddenly appeared in his host's eyes. He had seen it all too often in the gaze of determined mamas anxious to marry him to their eligible daughters. 'She is a most amusing *enfant*,' Ashley said, subtly emphasising the last word. 'I find her candour a trifle startling, but I overlook in a child what I would be dismayed by in an adult.' He was puzzled by Levisham's clear eagerness to have his beloved daughter marry when she herself strongly opposed it.

'She is so like her mama!' the Marquess exclaimed.

Ashley could not keep his disbelief from showing. Seeing it, Levisham explained, 'Not so much in looks, I grant you, for Caro has my colouring, but in character and vibrancy. Her mama could never curb her tongue either and used to say the most outrageous things.'

But Caro's mama had been a great beauty and the toast of the ton. Such an exquisite creature could have got away with much that a plainer girl could not. But apparently the Marquess did not realise that.

'Her mama was my sun, and moon, and stars.' Levisham's sunken face seemed to cave in more upon itself. 'After she died, I lost interest in everything but my children. I retired from society to nurse my grief and devote myself to bringing them up. I thought that here at Bellhaven I could protect them from any harm, from the evil and disease that plague the world. Only now do I see what a foolish hope that was. Death cannot be outwitted.'

Vinson looked sharply at his host's shrunken face and body. So Levisham was a dying man. What, Ashley wondered uneasily, would happen to Caro when her father was dead? Custom dictated that she become the ward of the new Marquess and head of the family, Tilford Kelsie, who was both a drunkard and a mama's boy. Furthermore, Ashley had not liked the way that bacon-faced Tilford had eyed Caro the previous night in the drawing room, rather like a hungry cat stalking a mouse.

What kind of life would poor Caro lead, once she no longer had her father to protect her?

CHAPTER EIGHT

WHEN ASHLEY finished dressing for dinner that night, he sent his valet on a reconnoitring mission. Swope returned with confirmation of his master's suspicion that Grace and Jane Kelsie, as they had the previous night, were again hovering just around the turn in the hall, waiting for him to emerge. Such over-eager females, no matter how lovely, disgusted Ashley.

Opening the door silently, he tiptoed down the hall in the opposite direction to the back stairs, and took them to the first floor. Heading toward the drawing-room, he heard, through the half-opened door of the dining-room, Olive Kelsie's shrilly raised voice. 'But I would *never* have locked dearest Caroline in her room! She is dreadfully mistaken.'

'Then how is it that the door was locked?' Levisham demanded.

'I am certain that it was not locked,' she said thinly. 'I do believe the door to her room sticks slightly. Yes,' she continued, her voice gaining strength from this inspiration, 'I am certain that is what must have happened. It stuck, and dearest Caroline thought that it was locked.'

'Then I shall have to have it checked frequently to make certain that it does not become stuck again. One other thing, Olive. Your seating arrangement for dinner did not suit me. I have changed it, and it will remain this way until our guests depart.'

As Ashley stepped into the drawing-room, the door to the dining-room opened, and he had a glimpse of Mrs Kelsie's face, red as a lobster in her rage.

When Grace and Jane came into the drawing-room, Ashley was gratified to see the startled chagrin upon their faces as they saw that he was already there. Little as he liked the two sisters, he had to admit that Grace looked exquisite in a frothy, beruffled creation of pink jaconet muslin.

Several minutes later, Caro came in, wearing a gown cut along exceedingly skimpy lines, as though the seamstress had been forced to conserve material. The result emphasised, rather than softened, her thin boyish figure. The neckline had been cut far too low for a child with her meagre endowment. Even worse was the gown's colour, a shade of pink that should have been prohibited on anyone of her colouring, for it made her look dreadfully sallow. Suddenly he realised that Caro's gown was of the identical pink jaconet as Grace's. His eyes moved from one cousin to the other, and a dark suspicion entered his mind.

Seeing Caro, her aunt hurried toward her with an evil look in her eye. Ashley, who was talking to Emily and Mercer, hastily excused himself to his companions and followed Mrs Kelsie.

'How dared you tell your father that I locked you in your room,' she hissed at her niece. Gone was the 'dearest Caroline' and the syrupy tone that Olive had affected whenever someone else was about.

'But I did not,' Caro began.

'Don't lie to me!' her aunt snapped.

'She is not lying,' Ashley interjected coldly.

Mrs Kelsie, who had thought herself out of earshot of everyone but her niece, whirled in consternation to face him.

'I am the one who told her father,' Ashley said, 'and he was as enraged as I thought he should be.'

Mrs Kelsie was so stunned that she convicted herself by gasping, 'How could you know?'

'My room is two doors from hers,' he replied. That much was true.

Caro's aunt immediately drew the conclusion that Ashley had intended her to. 'I assure you that your eyes deceived you, Lord Vinson. I was merely checking the key.'

'How odd that it should be the only room with the key on the outside of the door,' he observed. 'I will not scruple to tell you, Mrs Kelsie, that I found your action shocking. What if there had been—God forbid—a fire?'

Caro's aunt suddenly seemed to be experiencing a great deal of difficulty in breathing, and her face grew quite as red as it had been when she emerged from the dining-room. Without a word, she stalked off.

Caro turned grey eyes, shining with gratitude, to Ashley. 'How nice of you.'

'I wager you won't find yourself locked in again, so there is no need for you to climb down that tree tomorrow.'

'Oh, I would not have anyhow,' Caro said cheerfully. 'I gave Papa my word that I would not, and I would never break my word to him or to anyone.'

After dinner, Olive insisted on cards for entertainment and adroitly manoeuvred Ashley to a whist table that included Grace, Jane and Lord Sanley. To

Caro's acute unhappiness, her aunt assigned her to
be Tilford's partner, but her spirits picked up when
she saw that Emily and Mercer Corte would also be
at her table. Tilford was a wretched player, and the
way he kept eyeing Caro made her so nervous that
she could not keep her mind on the cards. They were
roundly defeated by their opponents, even though
Emily and Mercer were clearly more interested in each
other than in the card-play.

Caro had been dismayed when she had learned that
Emily wanted to marry Corte. But now that Caro had
met her friend's personable suitor, observing how
happy they were together and the adoring way that
they regarded each other, she understood for the first
time why a woman as intelligent as Emily might actually choose to wed. Emily's and Mercer's eyes met
repeatedly over their cards in such a speaking look of
mutual love and magnetism that Caro found herself
wondering what it would be like to be so obviously
loved and cherished by a man like him.

Or like Ashley? He was such charming company—
and nice, too. Not at all toplofty like Sanley or malicious like Sir Percival or sapskulled like Paul
Coleman. Their ride that morning had been capital
fun, and Caro would always be grateful to Ashley for
protecting her from Aunt Olive before dinner. That
meal, seated between him and her father, had been
one of the most entertaining that she could remember.

Looking out the window of his bedchamber the following morning, Ashley glanced apprehensively
towards the large elm that marked Caro's room. To
his relief, no tell-tale movement indicated that she was
not keeping her word to her father. A smile tugged

at Ashley's lips as he remembered how emphatic she had been that she would never break her word. The child might be a ramshackle hoyden, but she was a most entertaining one. He could appreciate why her father cherished her so. Life at Bellhaven would be considerably duller without her.

She had been seated between Ashley and Levisham at dinner the previous night, making the meal far more enjoyable than it had been on the Viscount's first night at Bellhaven when he had been stuck between her two boring cousins.

Ashley had been amused by the ill-concealed fury on Mrs Kelsie's face when she had seen the new seating arrangement that Levisham had dictated. At the opposite end of the table from Ashley, who was between Caro and Emily Picton, sat Tilford with his mother on one side and Grace on the other. Percy Plymtree and his creaking Cumberland corset had been placed between Grace and Jane.

Despite Levisham's retirement from society, he had maintained a keen interest in literature, the theatre, politics and affairs of state, which he had shared with his daughter. Ashley had been bemused by the intelligence with which Caro had discussed these subjects. She might be naïve, but she had a quick mind. Nor did she hesitate to disagree with him. He found her frank tongue diverting after all the simpering girls who hung on his every word. True, she wanted conduct, but he was less put off by her than he had been in the beginning.

Ashley looked out over the rolling green hills and woods of Bellhaven's park, invitingly serene in the soft light of morning. The spell of hot weather had not yet broken, and the day would again be scorching, making the park seem even more inviting. Breakfast would not be for another hour, and he decided to go for a stroll first.

Twenty minutes later he was standing before a particularly splendid weeping beech in the park, admiring the gracious droop of its branches, when he noticed a silver-haired terrier circling an elm in the distance. Then a flash of colour in the luxurious foliage of one of its lowest branches caught his eye. Abandoning his contemplation of the beech, he ran towards the elm, certain of what he would find when he reached it.

His foreboding again proved correct. Caro's tiny figure, clad in an old frock that was clearly a relic of her school-room days, its skirts tied up about her thighs to reveal legs encased in a beruffled pair of white drawers and feet in nankeen half-boots, was hidden in the greenery. To Ashley's relief, the branch that she had chosen was not far off the ground. She was talking, apparently to something in the tree with her, so softly that he could not hear her words.

Not wanting to startle her, Ashley took care to make a very noisy approach to the tree. The leaves parted, and her thin face appeared above him.

'Why is it, Caro, that I must always find you up a tree?' he asked in exasperation, feeling like a frustrated father trying to deal with a disobedient child.

'And why must *you* always rise so early?' she retorted with a gleam of mischievous humour.

'What the devil are you up to now?' His concern for her safety made his voice strident. 'You gave your word to your papa that you would no longer climb trees. Is this how you keep it?'

Laughter fled from the big grey eyes, and they flashed with indignation. 'I would never break my word. How ungentlemanly of you to accuse me of doing so. I promised Papa only that I would not use the elm as a staircase from my room. And I shan't!'

Ashley, wondering whether her father was aware of this distinction, repeated, 'What are you doing up there?'

'Rescuing Muffy.' She nodded her head towards her shoulder, which was obscured by the foliage. Ashley noticed for the first time a puff of white fur with dark markings, which proved to be a kitten fastened to her shoulder. 'That wretched dog scared her up the tree, and she was afraid to come down. There was nothing to be done but for me to climb up and rescue her.'

'You might have summoned one of the servants to do so.'

The big eyes were again indignant. 'But that would have taken for ever, and Muffy was so frightened. I could not have been so cruel as to leave her up here all that time, could I?'

Ashley diplomatically refrained from a truthful answer to this question, saying instead, 'Hand the creature down to me.'

But Muffy did not wish to be handed down. Instead, she clung tenaciously to her rescuer's shoulder. Finally Ashley instructed Caro to sit on the limb, which was only a foot or so above his head, and push off into his outstretched arms.

As he caught her and set her on the ground, he reflected again that she weighed no more than a feather. Muffy, frightened by this precipitous descent, was meowing furiously and digging her claws sharply into Caro's shoulder. But she did not seem to

mind the kitten's lack of gratitude. Instead, she
soothed it until it was purring happily.

The child was too soft-hearted for her own good,
Ashley thought unhappily. She needed a guardian, and
he seemed to be repeatedly trapped in that unwanted
role.

When the men rejoined the women in the drawing-
room that night, a small orchestra was setting up in
one corner to provide music. The furniture had been
temporarily pushed from that end of the room to
provide a small dance floor.

The day had been unbearably hot and humid, and
night had brought no relief. When Ashley came in,
he looked so cool and impeccable that Caro was instantly conscious of how hot and untidy she must
look. She glanced rather enviously at Grace, who was,
as always, perfectly groomed in a stylish yellow ba-
tiste gown with not a single hair out of place.

But to her surprise, it was not the lovely Grace that
Ashley sought out, but herself. He had scarcely
reached her, however, when Aunt Olive hurried up
with Grace and Jane.

'We are about to begin the dancing,' Aunt Olive
said, waving her fan coyly. 'My daughters tell me that
you are a superb dancer, putting all the other men
here in the shade.'

'Your daughters flatter me, ma'am,' Ashley replied
coolly, not looking at all like a man who was flattered.

The orchestra struck up. Both Grace and Jane
looked expectantly at Ashley, each clearly hoping that
she would be the one he asked to dance, but he turned
to Caro. 'Will you do me the honour of standing up
with me?'

As he swept her away, Caro had a hard time not to chuckle at the chagrin on her cousins' faces.

After their dance was over, he stood up with Emily, then with each of the other ladies in the room. After a second dance with Caro, he retired from the dance floor to engage his host in conversation, while Grace and Jane cast baleful looks in his direction.

The tall French doors that led out to the terrace had been opened wide in a vain attempt to cool the drawing-room. Fanning herself vigorously, Caro looked longingly beyond the doors at the night. Her despised fan was proving to be more utilitarian than useless tonight. When no one was watching, she glided out on the terrace, only to discover that one corner of it was already occupied.

Deep in protective shadows, Emily and Mercer were locked in an embrace. Remembering Tilford's loathsome kiss, Caro shuddered. Yet Emily clearly relished Mercer's.

That night, when the young ladies retired, Caro, beset by confusion, trailed Emily into her room. As her friend sat down at the dressing-table, Caro said, 'I saw you kissing Mercer tonight on the terrace.'

Emily's startled eyes met Caro's in the reflection of the mirror above the dressing-table. 'Did anyone else...?'

'No, you were well hidden. Do you like it?' Caro could not suppress a tiny shudder as she remembered Tilford's advances. 'I fear that I would find kissing a man exceedingly unpleasant.'

Emily smiled. 'That is only because you have never been in love. I promise you that when you lose your heart to a man, you will like his kisses very much.

Indeed, I predict that you will yearn for them as I do for Mercer's.'

Caro sincerely doubted that. Perhaps with Ashley, however... Suddenly, Caro found herself wondering what it would be like to be kissed by him. Could it be that she was not as immune to a man's charm as she had believed herself? Dismayed, she told herself not to be such a ninnyhammer, especially over a man who had his pick of beautiful women. Aloud, she protested fiercely, as though she were trying to convince herself as much as Emily, 'I shall never fall in love, nor marry either!'

Emily's slender fingers began to remove the pins from her hair. 'You seem to enjoy Lord Vinson's company.'

Caro, caught by surprise, confessed, 'I like him.' Then, lest Emily get the wrong idea, she added hastily, 'I wonder which of my cousins will catch him.'

'Neither will,' Emily said with certainty, her fingers still busy with her hairpins. 'Even Grace, lovely as she is, cannot hold a candle to the divine Lady Roxley.'

Caro could not stop herself from asking, 'Is it true what you said about his being more faithful to his mistress than most men are to their wives?'

Emily nodded. 'Vinson wanted desperately to marry her, but his father forbade it.'

This explanation of why he had not married his great love depressed Caro. 'I would not have thought him so lacking in bottom. He should have wed her, no matter what his father said.'

'He would have, but the lady rescinded her consent after his father threatened to cut him off without a ha'penny. Then she gave her hand to the richest man she could find.'

'You make her sound mercenary.'

'She is, but very clever at disguising it and at mesmerising gentlemen.'

Caro sighed. 'It is the same with Grace and Jane. The men do not see past their beauty to their shrewish natures. I feel sorry for Ashley if one of them captures him.'

Having dispensed with the hairpins that had bound her long sable hair, Emily began brushing it vigorously. 'Neither of your cousins has a chance, with Lady Roxley in Vinson's life.'

'Do not underestimate my aunt's and cousins' determination and tenacity.'

'Vinson is a master at eluding the designing mamas and their beautiful daughters.'

'My wager is on Aunt Olive,' Caro said, feeling strangely miserable at the prospect that Ashley might marry one of her cousins.

CHAPTER NINE

BY THE END of a week at Bellhaven, Ashley would have been the first to agree that Caro's faith in her aunt's tenacity was well founded. Although he was much practised at sidestepping such females with grace and good humour, Olive Kelsie and her offspring proved to be a enormous challenge not to his bachelorhood, for their aggressiveness served only to convince him that nothing would induce him to offer for either of them, but to his patience and good manners. He now knew, he thought ruefully, how a fox must feel with the hounds yapping at his heels.

Mrs Kelsie made so many oblique references to her daughters' superior understanding of marriage and the pleasures gentlemen often required outside its confines that Ashley was assured that his conversation on the terrace with Mercer Corte had been overheard.

Bad as Olive was, her younger daughter was even more obnoxious. Pouncing upon a possible way of outshining her more beauteous sister in Ashley's eyes, Jane told him, amid much fan-fluttering and coy glances, that Grace was so puffed in her estimation of her beauty that she would certainly be in a flame if ever she thought her husband might look at another woman.

'But I am not at all like her,' Jane continued, cornflower-blue eyes peeking demurely at him from above her fan. 'I understand how it is for some gentlemen, and I should never hold *my* husband to account.'

Ashley, certain that she would fly into as great a pelter as her sister, was so offended by her demeaning lie that he was sorely tempted to tell her that he did not doubt for a moment that *her* poor husband would wish to avail himself of her broad-mindedness.

To escape from Grace and Jane, Ashley sought Caro out with increasing frequency. Not only did the child have no designs on him, but she was amusing and, despite her naïveté, had a quick intelligence. Female accomplishments might elude her, but she had a number of unconventional ones—from her skill at billiards to her ability to hold her own in a lively argument with him—that made her by far the most entertaining of the seven young ladies on his father's list. How unfortunate that she should be such a hopelessly ineligible child!

Each day, Ashley accompanied Caro on early-morning horseback rides about the park. He won from her father permission for her to play billiards with him, thereby circumventing her outraged aunt. Ashley was held to be an outstanding player, but Caro was a worthy opponent. So worthy that the other male guests often gathered round to watch their matches.

Ashley's attention to Caro brought the ire of her aunt and cousins upon her. Grace, who saw only perfection when she looked in her mirror, warned Caro quite sincerely, 'Vinson is only trying to make me jealous. Do not think that he means anything by his feigned interest in you.'

'I do not,' Caro replied truthfully. She was perfectly aware that handsome Corinthians like Ashley did not fall in love with antidotes like herself. She had not led *that* sheltered a life.

'Yes, you do, you silly little fool,' Grace cried spitefully. She had long cursed an unjust fate that had wasted fortune and birth upon such a paltry girl as Caro instead of bequeathing it to her; she, with her great beauty, was far more deserving. 'You hope he means to make you an offer!'

'I do not!' Caro retorted, knowing that to be an impossibility. 'You know that I am determined never to marry!'

Grace's cornflower-blue eyes glittered cruelly. 'You say that only because no man would marry you except for your fortune.'

Grace was right. Never would a man look at Caro in the adoring way that Mercer Corte looked at Emily. The thought of what it would be like to have Ashley look at her that way made her knees grow weak for an instant before her good senses took hold and reminded her that she was a peagoose to think of such a thing.

Caro examined herself despairingly in her mirror. All her flaws seemed to leap out at her from her reflection: eyes too big, face too thin, skin too sallow. If only she could do something with her complexion and mousy, uncontrollable hair. She had wanted to have it cut short, but her aunt had objected strenuously, telling her father that it would make her look even less like a lady than she already did.

Having recently seen an advertisement that called Gowland's Lotion 'the most pleasant and effective remedy for all complaints to which the Face and Skin are liable,' Caro surreptitiously acquired a supply. Her

face and skin had so many problems that she would
be a true test of Gowland's claims.

For the first time in her life, she began to pay close
attention to her clothes, none of which, she thought
despairingly, seemed to make her look very attractive. She tried hard to act more ladylike, too,
walking at a slower pace and even fluttering her fan
occasionally.

Each morning, Caro would peer eagerly into her
mirror to see whether Gowland's Lotion had yet
changed her complexion for the better. And, each
morning, she was disappointed. Nevertheless, she
persevered in using it lavishly.

All of her efforts seemed to go for naught, too.
Inevitably, Ashley caught her in some childish caper
when she had momentarily reverted to her old ways.
It was positively perverse the way he managed to come
upon her when she was climbing an elm tree to rescue
Muffy again or when her father's hounds had just left
their enthusiastic welcome imprinted on her skirt. No
wonder Ashley thought her nothing more than an
amusing child.

One night Ashley asked Caro whether she would
like to ride in his curricle the following day so that
he could show her his chestnuts' paces. She hesitated,
then replied truthfully, 'I should like it above anything, but I fear that I must make my rounds
tomorrow.'

He raised a quizzical eyebrow. 'Your rounds, elfin?'

She explained that once a week she visited the ailing
among her father's tenants and dependants.

'Let me take you round,' Ashley volunteered.

'You will be bored,' Caro warned.

Not half so bored, he thought, as he would be trapped in her cousins' company. Smiling, he said gallantly, 'How could I be bored in your company, elfin?'

Her heart seemed to bump against her ribs. Determined to know the truth, she bluntly asked him why he was paying her so much attention.

'Except for Emily, who loves Mercer Corte, you are the only girl here that is not trying to legshackle me,' he told her. 'You, child, are my armour against the others.'

Caro was deeply wounded that Ashley saw her not as a woman, but only as an amusing child to be used as a shield against women who wanted to rivet him. Despite the lump in her throat, she managed to say lightly, 'Yes, you are quite safe with me.'

The following morning, Vinson was abruptly summoned to attend Levisham in his estate-room. When Ashley entered the chamber, the Marquess rose from behind his massive desk that half filled the small room and gestured to him to take a straight-backed chair. As Ashley complied, he was again struck by how frail his host looked.

'I shall waste no time, but go immediately to the reason that I called you here,' Levisham said abruptly, his directness reminding Ashley of his daughter. 'We each face serious dilemmas. I propose a solution that would solve both of them, I believe, to our mutual satisfaction.'

'I fear I do not comprehend,' Ashley said, at a loss to know what his host was talking about.

'You must wed, and I must marry off my daughter. If you were to wed her, it would solve both our problems.'

Ashley was so thunderstruck that he blurted, 'But Caro is a child!'

'A very temporary state,' Levisham replied calmly. 'Nevertheless, my only reason for marrying is to obtain an heir and a gracious chatelaine. A girl barely out of the schoolroom will not do.'

'I grant you that Caro is young for her age, but in no time she will make a lucky man as excellent a wife as her mama did me. I propose to make you that lucky man.'

'How very kind of you,' Ashley said drily, 'but why is it that Caro must be married off in such haste?'

'Because I fear that I do not have long to live. The fever that struck me last spring has weakened my heart. When I die, Caro, unless she is married, will become a ward of her cousin Tilford. She will be at the mercy of him and his evil mama, who will force her to marry him.'

'Good God!' Ashley exclaimed, horrified at the prospect of Caro being shackled to that drunken dolt. 'Why would your sister-in-law want such a union? It is clear that she does not even like your daughter.'

Levisham's lip curled contemptuously. 'Olive has two driving passions: ambition and greed. It is true that she detests my daughter, but she lusts for the great fortune that Caro inherited from her mother. Furthermore, Tilford cuts such a sorry figure that he is not likely to win the competition for any other great heiress.'

'His mother would not rest until she has squeezed every bit of spirit and liveliness out of Caro,' Ashley said in disgust. 'It cannot be permitted to happen.'

Levisham gave him an approving smile from across the broad desk. 'You have a quick understanding, like your father. The only way that I can ensure Caro escapes that fate is to see, before I die, that she is married to a man who will care for her properly, a somewhat older man who has the patience and experience to guide her with kindness and affection into adulthood.' Levisham fixed Ashley with a penetrating eye. 'I believe you are that man.'

Ashley shifted on the uncomfortable straight-backed chair. 'Why me?'

'I always had great admiration for your father, who was as honourable a man as I have ever met. I have made enquiries of you. Your character is as highly regarded as his. In addition, you have an amiable disposition and you like Caro, even though you are put off by her age. You are the only man I know that I am willing to trust my daughter to.'

'How flattering, but why the devil should *I* wed a hoydenish child?'

Levisham plucked a quill pen from the inkstand and absently smoothed its feather. 'Because you must marry, and Caro was on your father's list of acceptable young ladies.'

Ashley was horrified. Had everyone at Bellhaven overheard his conversation with Mercer Corte? How could he tell Levisham that the Earl of Bourn, whom he so greatly admired, would never countenance Caro as his heir's wife?

'I hardly need to remind you,' Levisham continued, 'that Caro's breeding is excellent and her fortune very large. Her husband will control it once she is married, for I dare not turn it over to her to squander.'

'Caro does not strike me as a spendthrift,' Ashley objected.

'She would not squander it on jewels, expensive gowns and other extravagances like most young women, but on the needy—and the unscrupulous. In her kind-hearted innocence, she had frequently been an easy mark for those with a sad, untrue tale.' Levisham's left hand continued alternately to ruffle and smooth the feather of the pen that he held in his right. 'She is constitutionally incapable of resisting anyone who sheds a tear in her presence, and must be protected from her own generosity.'

'I might waste her wealth,' Ashley warned.

Levisham gave him a shrewd smile. 'You might, but you won't. In fact, you would manage it prudently and for her benefit, would you not?'

'Yes, of course I would,' Ashley said impatiently. 'But it is not a responsibility I seek. Nor do I want to wed a child, and most particularly one who does not wish to marry me or any other man.'

Levisham sighed. 'I fear that my own selfishness is much to blame for that. She is so much like her dear mama that I could not bear the thought of losing her to a husband. I encouraged her distaste for marriage, which was not difficult. This neighbourhood offers several unfortunate examples of the misery that can befall a wife. Caro, who cannot bear to see another suffer, took their experiences much to heart.' The Marquess dipped the point of his pen into the inkpot and began doodling absently on a sheet of paper. 'But I have seen the way she looks at you, and I am certain that in time you could, if you were of a mind to, capture her heart. You are reputed to make love charmingly.'

'I hardly think *that* would win the approval of a prospective father-in-law,' Ashley said grimly. 'Furthermore, if you overheard my talk with Mercer Corte, which I think you must have to be aware of my father's list, you must also know that there is another woman in my life.'

'Yes, I know about your mistress,' Levisham said calmly.

'Since we are speaking plainly, Caro deserves better than a husband who loves his mistress.'

'Yes,' her father agreed, 'but she insists that she wants a marriage in which her husband has another interest.'

'But, my lord,' Ashley cried, profoundly shocked, 'whatever your daughter's naïve sentiments may be, surely my attachment must make me ineligible in *your* eyes?'

'Not at all. In truth, I prefer it, too.'

Ashley's jaw dropped. This was not a conversation he would ever have envisioned having with a prospective father-in-law. 'Good God, why?'

'A man with other interests will make fewer demands on her.' The Marquess's face clouded, and the pen slid unnoticed from his fingers. 'She is as tiny and delicate as her mama.'

Tiny perhaps, Ashley thought, but Caro was about as delicate as a steel rod.

'And too young and fragile for endless child-bearing.' Levisham's face suddenly sagged with grief, and his voice broke. 'Just as her mama was when we married. But I had such a passion for her that I could not keep my hands off her.' His voice dropped to an agonising whisper. 'Childbirth and miscarriages sapped her health, and she died giving birth to Caro's little sister, who lived but forty-eight hours.'

'So, if I were to marry Caro, you prefer to have me in my mistress's bed rather than my wife's,' Ashley said sharply. 'While I have no wish to turn my wife into a brood mare, I must remind you that the reason I must marry is for an heir.'

'But once she has given you that...' Levisham broke off, asking abruptly, 'Whom else on your father's list would you prefer to marry?'

The question silenced the Viscount, for the answer was clearly 'No one'.

Levisham smiled shrewdly. 'You see! And I promise you that Caro will never raise any objection to your mistress.'

'I think you are wrong about that, and that is why I cannot marry her.' Ashley had come to feel like a protective big brother to Caro. He was too fond of her to offer her a marriage that would hold no happiness for her.

'I know my daughter very well, and I assure you that she will not object. You said that if you found such a woman, you would marry her.'

Yes, Ashley had said that, but Caro deserved better. 'I cannot...'

Levisham silenced him with a wave of his hand. 'How can you be so cruel as to consign her to Tilford and Olive Kelsie? Do not give me your answer yet. Think about it for a few days.'

CHAPTER TEN

IT WAS a subdued, thoughtful Ashley who took Caro on her calls later that morning, but she seemed not to notice as she told him about the people they were to meet. He was surprised by how much she knew of the history and families, the pleasures and problems of her father's tenants and retainers.

Ashley was struck by the genuine affection that the people they visited had for Caro, and by hers for them. He was struck, too, by how good she was with the children and the ill. There was a maturity about her in these moments that he had not seen before.

One of their stops was at the cottage of a tenant farmer whose five-year-old son was slowly recuperating from scarlet fever. Little more than skin and bones, he lay listlessly on a narrow straw bed in a corner of the cottage's one room.

The abode was clean, its bare stone floor well swept and scrubbed, but sparsely furnished. A long trestle table of rough pine, flanked by two benches, took up the middle of the room. Ashley suspected that an old, much scarred pine chest against one wall held the family's entire wardrobe. The wall across from it was dominated by a stone fireplace with cooking-pots upon its brick hearth. A roughly-woven curtain had been drawn around the corner opposite the boy's pallet to hide his parents' bed.

The child's blue eyes, still dull from his illness, lighted with joy at the sight of Caro. She had brought him a top, striped with green and yellow and red, to play with and a basket of delicacies from Bellhaven's kitchen to tease his nonexistent appetite. She coaxed him into letting her feed him while she enthralled him with lively tales about knights and dragons.

Ashley, who sat down on one of the benches at the rough trestle table, enjoyed Caro's imaginative bent for storytelling as much as the boy did.

'A miracle it is, the way he eats for her,' the child's appreciative mother told Ashley. 'She has a way with little ones. A dear, kind-hearted girl, she is.' The woman's face darkened. 'But there are those who would take advantage of her kindness.'

Ashley remembered what Levisham had said about Caro being the prey of frauds.

'Innocent little thing can never resist tears, and there be some who would cry to her, not from trouble but for gain!'

When Caro rose from the boy's bedside to leave, he clutched at her hand until she promised that she would come back another day and tell him more stories.

Later, after Caro and Ashley were back in his curricle, she asked, 'May I handle the ribbons?'

He turned them over to her, and she proved to be a natural and daring driver. Watching her, Ashley nodded approvingly. Another one of her unconventional, but very real, accomplishments.

Only once did she get into trouble, and that was not her fault. As they rounded a curve on a narrow stretch of road at a fast pace, they met a cart, piled high with corn, hogging the roadway.

Ashley grabbed the reins. It required all his skill to miss the vehicle and keep his own upright. He was forced to drive partly off the road, and Caro was thrown against him. Reflexively his arm shot round her to hold her protectively against him. When he again had the curricle under control, he looked down at her frightened face, which seemed all big grey eyes and provocatively opened lips.

Their gazes met for an electric moment, and Ashley was nearly overcome by a temptation, as strong as it was surprising, to kiss her. But, remembering the revulsion that she had expressed to him the day they had met, he reluctantly quelled his urge and removed his arm. It would not do to frighten her.

Until today Ashley had thought of Caro only as as entertaining child, but accompanying her on calls had given him a very different view of her. No longer did he doubt her father's prediction that she would eventually make a man an excellent wife, *if she wished to marry him*. What irony that she wanted to wed no more than Ashley himself did. If he accepted her father's proposal, would she even agree to marry him?

As the curricle came into sight of Bellhaven, Ashley said thoughtfully, 'You are so good with children that I do not understand why you do not wish to wed and have your own.'

Pain flashed in her eyes for an instant before her delicate chin rose defiantly. 'I am determined to remain a spinster and devote myself to Papa, as Abigail Foster did. Not that her father was worthy of her! Indeed, I do not understand how she could have been so devoted to such a demanding, ungrateful curmudgeon!'

'I apprehend, elfin, that you did not like him.'

Caro's grey eyes flashed angrily. "No, I did not! Indeed of rewarding her for her devotion to him, he tipped her the double.'

Ashley's brows rose questioningly. 'How?'

'Abigail turned down several handsome offers to devote herself to him, and he promised to provide her with an independent income on his death so that she might set up her own household. Instead, when his will was read, it was found that he had placed her portion under her brother's control until she marries, which, of course, she never will. Surely her father must have known how it would be for Abigail with her brother's odious wife.'

'Her brother lives under the cat's paw, does he?'

Caro nodded her head in vigorous assent. 'He is very nearly as henpecked as my poor uncle was by Aunt Olive.'

'What did the odious wife do to Abigail?' Ashley asked, firmly holding his chestnuts to a trot.

'Had her packed off to Scotland to live with a cantankerous old aunt, whom Abigail has always cordially disliked.'

Ashley's face tightened into a frown. An even worse fate would await Caro if she were not married before her father died. 'So Abigail now finds herself in the very situation that she had sought to escape by not marrying.' His voice was suddenly brusque. 'She might have wed a man who would have made her very happy. Remember her, elfin, when you would reject any thought of matrimony.'

She looked at him with puzzled eyes before she said briskly, 'It does not signify, for no man is likely to want to marry me.'

* * *

When Olive Kelsie learned that Caro and Ashley had gone off together in his curricle, she flew into a pucker. It was beyond her comprehension that Ashley could have any interest in her plain, hoydenish niece, but if that were the case it would ruin her carefully laid plans for both her son and daughters.

Her unease grew when she learned that Ashley had been closeted with Levisham prior to departing with Caro. Indeed, Olive had not been so alarmed since she had feared that Levisham, after his son's death, meant to offer for Abigail Foster. The thought that he might do so and breed another son, thereby cutting her darling Tilford out of his rightful inheritance, had been enough to reduce Mrs Kelsie's iron constitution to palpitations.

Even though Miss Foster's opposition to matrimony was well known, Mrs Kelsie had long suspected that Abigail harboured a secret *tendre* for Levisham, which had been her real reason for rejecting her suitors.

Determined to have this dangerous threat removed, Olive had convinced Miss Foster's self-important sister-in-law that she would never be mistress of her new home while Abigail continued to reside there.

When Caro and Ashley returned, Olive, grimly determined to end this latest threat to her ambitions, immediately launched a concerted campaign to point out all 'dearest Caroline's' defects to Ashley. Olive did not overlook the smallest detail, from her niece's flyaway hair and her brown complexion to her scrawny figure and the scuffed toes on her half-boots.

But despite Olive's best—and frequently repeated—efforts, her aspersions did not have their desired effect on Ashley, whom she was beginning to find quite as vexing and unmanageable as her brother-in-law. Worse, since Vinson had begun lavishing attention on Caro, the other gentlemen in the party paid much more attention to her, too. Only Sanley and Plymtree, still nursing their grudges against her, ignored her in favour of Mrs Kelsie's daughters.

On the night before the guests were to leave Bellhaven, Olive, seeking to display Grace and Jane to their best advantage, made them entertain the guests with a musical presentation. Both young ladies had pretty voices that won vigorous applause from their audience.

As they ended their performance, Olive insisted that Caro sing for their guests. The contrast between her niece, whom Olive knew could not sing a note, and her own daughters would surely give the audience a disgust of her.

Caro, whose lack of musical talent was a source of great embarrassment to her, turned as white as Ashley's stock. She tried to decline, but her aunt persisted. She was soon joined in her urgings by the polite, unsuspecting guests.

At last, seeing no hope of escape, Caro reluctantly stood before the guests, her knees shaking so that she wondered whether they would continue to support her through the humiliating ordeal ahead of her.

The faces before her seemed to be receding in a black haze of panic, and Caro longed for Providence to send a bolt from above to strike her dead before she had to open her mouth.

But Providence did not hear her silent plea.

Suddenly Ashley was at her side, towering above her. 'I have been seized by an irresistible urge to sing, too,' he said loudly. 'Pray, Lady Caro, be so kind as to let me join you in a duet.'

'Of course,' she stammered.

With an understanding squeeze, he took her icy hand in his warm one, smiled encouragingly at her, and said under his breath so that only she could hear, 'Sing softly, elfin, and I will carry you.'

She obeyed, and he proceeded to drown her sour notes with his fine baritone. Slowly, the shaking in her knees subsided, and her hand, still held firmly in his comforting clasp, warmed. Blessed Providence had sent her a far happier alternative to a bolt of lightning.

When they finished, the applause for them was as warm as it had been for her cousins. Never had Caro felt such overwhelming gratitude to anyone as she did at that moment to Ashley.

He led her to a small settee, just large enough for the two of them. As Caro sat down, she saw that her aunt was looking as though she had just swallowed a toad.

Glancing up at Ashley's smiling face, Caro thought with aching heart what a very, very lucky woman Lady Roxley was.

CHAPTER ELEVEN

ASHLEY, wandering in Bellhaven's park, chose a path that meandered through a wood into a green glade brightened by colourful clumps of goldenrod, purple knapweed and ox-eye daisies. He scarcely noticed the beauty about him or the yellow brimstone butterfly that fluttered in front of him, for he was contemplating the negative answer that he must soon give Levisham.

Most of the guests had already departed from Bellhaven; the others would be gone by the time Ashley returned to the house. He was impatient to return to London to begin his search for the one-eared man that Mercer Corte had seen with Henry. But Ashley would be the last to leave Bellhaven, because he had been procrastinating about rejecting the Marquess's offer of Caro's hand.

The Viscount's brows knitted in an unhappy frown. Although he liked Caro, she was clearly not the wife for him. He needed a cool, sophisticated lady of the first respectability, preferably a beauty, but if not that, at least a woman of great decorum who would serve as his charming chatelaine. It was what his father expected of him.

No, Ashley could not marry her.

The heat that had broken for a few days had returned with a vengeance. Ashley, feeling quite wilted from it, was irresistibly drawn toward the soothing sound of rushing water. It came from a stream that twisted sharply through this remote corner of the park, its water shaded from the merciless sun by a leafy green parasol of graceful willow branches.

When he reached the bank, he discovered that he was not alone. A slim little figure that he recognised instantly as Caro was gliding expertly through the water. From the pile of clothing lying on a flat rock, he suspected that she must be wearing nothing more than her shift.

Far more unsettling to Ashley was the sight of another figure partly concealed in the stripling birches and tall plants that grew in profusion along the water. Tilford Kelsie was watching Caro so intently that he had not noticed the newcomer. The cruelly lecherous look on Tilford's face both shocked and revolted Ashley.

The Viscount glanced again at Caro, who was cutting cleanly through the water with deft strokes. Silently, taking care to make no noise, he circled behind Caro's cousin. The sight of an empty claret-bottle lying at Tilford's feet disgusted Ashley. He caught the man from behind, jerked him round, and grabbed him by the lapels of his coat.

Tilford's breath reeked of wine, and his eyes bulged with fear as he saw the lethal look on Vinson's face. In a low, menacing voice, Ashley told him, 'Get out of here immediately, or I shall give you a beating that you will never forget. Then I shall go to the Marquess.'

The fear on Tilford's face told Ashley that he was a coward as well as a drunk. 'I'll go,' he whimpered.

'Don't stop until you reach the house,' Ashley ordered, releasing him.

Tilford stumbled clumsily away, trampling viciously underfoot the teasel's and the comfrey's delicate clusters of flowers.

'Who's there?' Caro's frightened voice called from the water.

Ashley turned and strode down to the water's edge. As he emerged from the screen of greenery, the alarm on her face, all that was visible above the surface, gave way to what appeared to be chagrin, and she cried in a mortified tone, 'Oh, Ashley, why must you always come upon me at the most awkward moments?'

'Why must you always put yourself in awkward situations?' he snapped, venting his anger at Tilford on her. 'Are you lost to all sense of propriety?'

He saw in her big grey eyes the same flash of pain that he had seen when he had been so shocked upon learning her identity. This time, however, there was no brave little smile. Instead, she asked in a small, perplexed voice, 'What has put you in such a tweak, Ashley? It is not like you.'

No, it was not like him, but he had no intention of standing on a river bank and explaining some unpleasant facts of life to this naïve infant. 'Never mind,' he said curtly. 'I'll escort you back to the house.'

'But I cannot go now,' she protested.

'Why not?'

A red flush of embarrassment spread over her face. 'I am wearing only my shift, and I—I thought I would dry myself in the sun. It is so remote here; I don't see how you found it. No one ever comes here.'

No one except her lecherous cousin! Angrily, Ashley's fingers went to his elegantly tied neckcloth and unwound the length of muslin. He dropped it on the rock beside her clothes. 'Here, use this to dry yourself. I will go back up the bank and turn my back until you are dressed.'

'Thank you, but I prefer to remain here,' she said politely.

'Caro,' he said in a furious voice, 'I am not leaving without you. Do not strain my patience.'

She regarded him with puzzled, hurt eyes. 'I do not understand why you are in such a pelter.'

The answer to that, he realised with sudden clarity, was far more complicated than she could have imagined. He had been resolved to reject her father's proposition, but how could he live with himself if he damned the poor child to that wretched Tilford? This quandary sorely ruffled his temper, and again he vented it on Caro. 'If you do not come out of the water,' he snapped at her, 'I shall be obliged to come in and fetch you. Pray do not make me do that.'

She did not, and a short time later they were returning to the house, her wet shift wrapped in his equally wet neckcloth. He was thankful that the guests would be gone by the time they reached the house. Otherwise his missing neckcloth and Caro's bedraggled appearance would have given rise to considerable gossip.

He studied her pixyish face. Although he had no wish to marry her, at least life with her would not be boring. But he did not love her. And, dammit, she deserved a man who would love her as she ought to be loved, who would cherish her as the only woman in his life. Ashley could not do that.

The memory of the brutish, lustful look on Tilford's face as he watched Caro swimming rose up to haunt Ashley. She already found the idea of lovemaking re-

pulsive. Her drunken cousin would confirm that her
fear had been well founded. And her aunt would rule
as mistress in Tilford's house. Ashley knew exactly
what sort of treatment poor Caro would receive at
Olive's hands.

This succession of unhappy thoughts left Vinson
scowling and silent as they walked back to the house.
In deference to his black mood, Caro grew very quiet,
too.

As they neared the house, Ashley's valet hurried
towards them. When the sharp-eyed Swope failed to
notice that his master's neckcloth, upon which he had
lavished so much attention that morning, was missing,
Ashley knew that something had to be dreadfully
wrong.

CHAPTER TWELVE

SWOPE immediately confirmed his employer's dark
surmise. The Marquess had been taken ill and wished
to see him immediately.

'What is wrong with Papa?' Caro cried in alarm.

Swope looked uncomfortable. 'I cannot say, except
that the doctor has been sent for,' he replied evasively.

Despite her tan, Caro suddenly looked very pale.
She started for the house at a run.

Ashley, certain that his valet knew more than he
had been willing to tell Caro, paused to ask again the
nature of the Marquess's illness.

Glancing around to make certain that Caro was out
of earshot, Swope said, 'I was told it is his heart. He
was stricken with excruciating chest pains shortly after
a, er, rather violent dustup with Mrs Kelsie.'

'What was that about? Don't tell me you couldn't
say, because I know you can.' Swope, who loved
gossip, could be counted on to pluck every titbit to
be had from the servant's grapevine.

'Her son stole a bottle of the Marquess's claret.
Also, Mrs Kelsie apparently attempted to humiliate
Lady Caroline last night. His lordship was heard to
tell Mrs Kelsie to get out and never set foot on
Bellhaven soil again while he was alive. A good deal
of commotion ensued.'

Ashley could well imagine that it had. 'How bad is
the Marquess's attack?'

Swope frowned. 'I heard he might stick his spoon to the wall.'

'Good God!' Ashley exclaimed. Looking towards the house, he saw that Caro was nearly there. He ran after her, following her inside and up the stairs to her father's bedchamber. When she tried to enter, Levisham's valet barred her way, saying that his lordship had been emphatic about wishing to see Lord Vinson before anyone else.

The Viscount knew that the Marquess wanted an answer about whether he would marry Caro. Until a short time ago, Ashley had intended to refuse. But the lascivious look on Tilford's face as he watched his unsuspecting cousin swimming had undermined Ashley's resolve.

When Ashley went in, Levisham was lying against the pillows. He attempted to raise his head, but it fell back weakly.

'Thank God they have found you,' he said, desperation in his rasping voice. 'I fear that I am dying... I must have your answer now...'

With a sinking heart, Ashley realised what that answer must be. His conscience would not permit him to abandon Caro to Tilford's untender mercies.

The Marquess paused as though trying to marshal his strength to go on. 'I promise you that Caro will meet your principal requirement for a wife. She will never plague you about Lady Roxley.'

'I do not believe that your daughter will be happy about such a marriage,' Ashley said sharply, thinking again that Caro deserved so much better.

'It is the very kind of marriage that she wants.'

'She might think so in the abstract, but I am persuaded that faced with the reality of it, she will not like it at all.'

'But she will,' Levisham grimaced as though torn by pain. 'She is still more child than woman, and she has some silly prejudices about men and marriage that must be dispelled. What is required is a husband who treats her with patience and gentleness and forbearance.' Again the Marquess's face contorted with pain. It was a long moment before he continued in a weak, halting voice. 'Meanwhile, you will have your mistress . . . All that I ask on that score is that . . . you do not ignore Caro . . . nor mortify her with too flagrantly open a liaison.'

'If you believe that I would treat my wife so callously, you should not be proposing to give your daughter to me,' Ashley said. 'Nor will I wed a woman against her will. If Caro objects to this arrangement, I cannot marry her.'

'If she does not object . . . you will wed her?'

'Only if she assures me that she wishes this arrangement,' Ashley emphasised.

Levisham's eyes glittered angrily, clearly taking silent umbrage at Vinson's insistence that Caro freely agree to their union.

Given her distaste for marriage, she would not like it, but she likely would agree to it, finding him preferable to her drunken cousin. Nevertheless, Ashley wanted to be certain that was the case. But why should her father be upset that the Viscount wanted Caro's assurance that she would not find marriage to him repugnant? Had she already told her father that she would?

Startled and a little uneasy about Levisham's odd reaction, Ashley said sharply, 'I reiterate that if she objects to...'

'I swear to you that she will not,' her father said coldly. 'Not to marrying you or to your relationship with Lady Roxley.'

'With all due respect, my lord, it is her oath, not yours, that I wish to hear,' Ashley said grimly. 'And I must hear it from her own lips. I insist on being private with her, just the two of us.'

'That is not necessary,' Levisham replied in furious accents.

'I insist on it!'

'Very well, then, you shall have her word,' the Marquess responded, clearly outraged.

Ashley stared at the Marquess, baffled by his anger.

Levisham closed his eyes wearily. 'You will be married tonight.'

'But that is impossible,' Ashley protested. 'We shall have to obtain a special licence.'

'I have already done so. All that remains to be done is for the minister to be summoned.'

More than a little exasperated at Levisham's presumption, Ashley said firmly, 'I must notify my parents. I do not wish to be married without them here.'

'By that time, I most likely will be dead. Do not deny me my last wish—to see my daughter safely married. Furthermore, if you insist on waiting for them to arrive, you may not be married at all. Count on my evil sister-in-law to find a way of preventing it once I am dead. You must marry immediately.'

'Yes,' Ashley said, thinking that perhaps haste was preferable from his own point of view, too. His father would not approve of Caro as a future Countess of Bourn. Much as Vinson hated to be married without his parents present, it would be easier to have the deed done before his father could kick up a storm over his choice of bride. It would mean, however, that Ashley must postpone his return to London and his search for the truth about William's death. He could not like that, but there was no helping it.

'Very well, we'll wed tonight,' he capitulated, 'but only if Caro assures me privately that this arrangement meets her approval.'

Once again anger flashed in Levisham's eyes. Seeking to soothe him, Ashley said, 'I promise that I shall take very good care of your daughter.' And he would. Now that he had agreed to the match, he was feeling much better about it. He could not have lived with himself had Caro fallen into Tilford's hands. She would be far happier as Ashley's wife. He would make certain of that. He was determined to be the patient, forbearing husband that Levisham wanted for his daughter.

The Marquess said, 'I ask one small favour of you.'

'Certainly; you have but to name it,' Ashley replied.

'Let Caro remain here with me. I have no one else. I do not want to die alone.'

The Viscount frowned. He did not want to deny a dying man's request, but Levisham could linger for weeks, and Ashley must return to London to search for the one-eared man. It was even more important that he find him now that he was marrying. If Henry had murdered William in order to inherit the earldom, everyone who stood in his way was in danger, especially Caro, who, should she become pregnant, would give birth to a new impediment. 'I have important business to attend to. I cannot remain at Bellhaven above a few days.'

'What can be that important?' Levisham demanded harshly.

For a moment Ashley considered telling him about Henry and the threat he might pose to Caro, but decided against it. What point was there in burdening a dying man with yet another worry? 'It is a personal matter.'

Levisham raised his hand from the coverlet in an indifferent gesture. 'Then depart when you wish, but leave Caro with me. You will have your mistress to occupy you in London.'

Ashley's frown deepened. 'There will be gossip.'

'Once it is known that Caro remained here because I am dying, it will be seen as the dutiful thing to do.'

'She may stay,' Ashley agreed with a rueful little smile. It would do him no good to tell her that she could not remain with her father. He knew his future bride well enough to be certain that nothing would prise Caro from her father's side now.

When the door closed behind Ashley, Levisham sat up abruptly, the weakness he had exhibited in the Viscount's presence gone.

The Marquess was not dying yet. But with his heart as bad as it was, his pretence could become a reality at any moment, and he had to get Caro safely married before that happened. It had been clear that Vinson intended to reject the offer of her hand, and Levisham had hit on a feigned deathbed scene as the most expedient way of obtaining both Caro's and Ashley's agreement to the marriage. His daughter would be stubborn, too, but he would enlist Dr Baxter's aid in bringing her round.

Not that he was happy about her marrying Vinson. He silently cursed a cruel fate that forced him to make Caro marry a man whose chief requirement in a wife was that she not object to his mistress.

When he was with Caro, Ashley gave every indication of being both fond and protective of her. He had moved swiftly the previous night to save her from Olive's attempt to humiliate her. Yet now, he was subjecting her to another kind of humiliation by requiring that she promise him she would not object to his mistress. As Vinson himself had said when the Marquess had proposed the match, 'Caro deserves better than a husband who loves his mistress.'

Levisham had seen the way that Caro looked at Ashley. Although she might not realise it yet, her heart was engaged by the handsome Viscount.

Which made it all the more painful to her father that he must insist that she give Ashley the demeaning promise he wanted. The Marquess had been so outraged by the Viscount's demand that he, in turn, had used the fiction that he was on his deathbed to induce Ashley to let Caro remain at Bellhaven. What need had Vinson for her in London when all he wanted was to rush back there to his mistress as quickly as possible after his wedding? No, he did not deserve Caro.

Levisham's head fell back wearily against the pillows. Poor Caro. It would be easy for Vinson to make her adore him. But would he return her affection? Or did he love Lady Roxley too much to ever be weaned from her?

CHAPTER THIRTEEN

CARO paced the hall outside her father's bedchamber anxiously waiting for Ashley to emerge. It was a measure of how much she had come to care for the Viscount that despite her overwhelming concern for her father, her hurt and bafflement over why Ashley had been so angry at her this morning still gnawed at her.

When at last he came into the hall, he looked at her gravely, a peculiar expression that she could not fathom in his green eyes. But all he said to her was, 'You may go in now.' His voice, too, sounded odd.

She rushed into the room, stopping abruptly at the sight of her father lying weakly against the white linen of the bed pillows, looking wretchedly unhappy.

'Is there anything I can do for you, Papa?' she cried.

He regarded her even more gravely than Ashley had in the hall. It was as though he were trying to decide how to tell her something of the utmost importance. At last, he said weakly, 'Yes, my pet, there is one thing you could do that would relieve my mind and make me feel much better.'

'Tell me, and I'll do it,' she cried eagerly.

He seemed reluctant to answer her. Caro, anxious to do anything she could that might ease him, pressed, 'What is it that you wish, Papa?'

'For you to marry.'

She disbelieved her ears. 'Surely,' she exclaimed, 'you are joking, Papa.' But even as she spoke, Caro

119

knew from his sombre expression that he was not. 'You know I do not want that,' she said reproachfully. 'I wish to devote myself to you.'

'That is very noble, my pet, but it is time that we faced the truth. I am not likely to live very much longer, and...'

'Don't say that!' she cried, throwing her arms about him as though to ward off death itself. Tears streamed down her cheeks at the thought of losing him.

He held her to him, stroking her hair and trying to comfort her as she sobbed out her grief. Her father had always been the foundation of her world, and she was certain that it would collapse if he died. Indeed, she could not imagine her life without him. She would have no one.

When Caro at last regained some semblance of composure, he told her bluntly, 'It is not for me that you should be weeping, but for yourself if I should die before you are married and settled.'

Caro, who had never before considered what would happen to her in that event, looked at him uncomprehendingly. 'What do you mean?'

'You will become your cousin Tilford's ward, because he will be the head of the family and your only living male relative. There is no one else.'

Caro, remembering with revulsion the incident in the stables, was terrified at the thought of living beneath her cousin's roof without her father to protect her.

'His mother will rule him and Bellhaven,' the Marquess continued. 'Your life with that pair would be exceedingly miserable.' Her father stroked her hair, which hung loose about her shoulders, still damp from her swim. 'Eventually they would force you to marry Tilford.'

'Oh, no!' Caro cried in horror, the sickening memory of her cousin's brutal advance engulfing her. To be his wife, to be continually subjected to such treatment, was more than she could bear to contemplate. 'I would rather be dead!' she cried passionately.

'I cannot say that I blame you,' her father said softly, still stroking her hair. 'We must foreclose the possibility of such a marriage.'

'How?' Caro asked desperately. She would do anything to escape from Tilford.

'By your marrying someone else before I die. I have found a man who understands your situation and has agreed to marry you in exchange for an assurance from you.'

Her head jerked up, and she gaped at him. 'Who?'

'Lord Vinson.'

Her father's face receded in a blur. The sudden flash of happiness that Caro had felt initially at the thought of marrying Ashley quickly vanished as she remembered Lady Roxley. 'But, Papa, he cannot want to marry me,' she protested. 'He—he has a lady to whom he is much attached.'

'No, he does not *want* to marry you any more than you do him, but he is willing to do so,' her father said bluntly.

'Why?' Caro asked. All of her cousins' oft-repeated assurances that no man would wed her except for her fortune returned to haunt her. 'For my money?'

'No, he is not a fortune-hunter!' Levisham exclaimed. 'Rest easy on that score. His inheritance will be as large as yours.'

'Then why is he willing to marry me, if not for money?'

The Marquess sighed. 'Vinson must marry—his father insists on it—and the lady you mentioned is already wed to another. He needs a wife to give him an heir, and you need a husband to save you from your aunt and Tilford. So, what could be better than that you marry each other?'

No wonder Ashley had looked at her so strangely in the hall. 'I cannot conceive why he should agree to marry me when so many far lovelier women yearn to be his wife,' she observed with characteristic honesty.

'He wants a wife who will not object to his relationship with Lady Roxley,' Levisham replied. 'You told me that the only marriage you would consider was one like Lady Fraser's, and so I have arranged precisely what you wanted.'

Or what Caro had thought she wanted before she had seen Emily and Mercer together, had seen how it could be between a man and woman who truly loved each other. And before she had met Ashley and discovered that her heart was not immune to a man. But he would never love her the way Mercer loved Emily. Beautiful Lady Roxley held his heart captive.

'You should be delighted that I have persuaded Vinson to save you from your aunt and cousin,' Levisham was saying.

Yes, she supposed that she should be, but she was not. Caro wondered what her father had had to do to win the Viscount's acquiescence. Was that why Ashley had been so angry with her this morning? 'What persuasion did you have to employ?'

'Vinson's principal requirement in a wife is that she not interfere with him and his other connection. I assured him that you would never object or even take the least notice of that.'

Caro's heart felt as though it were sinking into nether regions from which it would never escape. Her mutinous emotions must have reflected on her face, because her father cried in sudden agitation, 'You must never, under any circumstance, vex Vinson about Lady Roxley. Swear to me, Caro, that you will not. It is crucial. I think he is inclined to be fond of you, but nothing would sink his affection more quickly.'

Fearing that such perturbation was very bad for her father, Caro tried to calm him by saying, 'I swear, Papa. Only, please, do not fret yourself.'

His head sank back on the pillows. 'When you see Vinson, you must give him your solemn word on that score.'

Caro struggled to hide the shame that his request caused her. What if she refused? Would Ashley refuse to marry her, thereby consigning her to Tilford?

'Promise me that you will give Vinson your oath when you see him,' her father insisted.

'Yes, Papa,' she agreed reluctantly, afraid of the effect it would have upon him if she did not.

'Don't look so unhappy, my pet,' her father pleaded. 'Vinson is a man of superior manners and understanding. I am certain that he will treat you always with the utmost kindness and consideration if you do not plague him about his other interest. I own I do not believe that I could find a better man for you. You will not be mistreated like Clara Potter or Mrs Burke or Amelia Coleberd.'

No, Caro realised sadly, she had no fear that Ashley would abuse her—he was too decent for that—only that he would ignore her. She could not be optimistic about her future with a man who would marry her only because she would not object to his continuing affair with his true love.

'If you strive to be the kind of wife Vinson wants, my pet, he might in time come to love you,' Levisham said musingly, surveying her so critically that she wished she had taken the time to fasten up her long hair, still hanging loose about her shoulders. 'How untidy you look! You must take far greater pains with your appearance when you are Lady Vinson. You must learn to look and act like a lady. No longer can you indulge in hoydenish scraps or behaviour that would embarrass your husband.'

'Yes, Papa,' Caro said dully. He sounded like Aunt Olive. She would try very hard to be the kind of wife Vinson wanted, but she was pessimistic about her success in this endeavour.

'Vinson has agreed that you can be married tonight.'

'Tonight! Oh, no, Papa! I cannot, I *will* not leave you when you are so ill!'

'You will not have to. Vinson is amenable to your remaining here when he returns to London.'

And to Lady Roxley, Caro thought bleakly, sorely wounded that he would be willing to leave his new bride so quickly.

A knock on the door signalled the arrival of Dr Baxter, a greying, middle-aged man of considerable erudition beyond medicine. He had been one of her father's few intimates during his reclusive years at Bellhaven.

Caro was sent from the room while the doctor examined her father. She hovered outside, her thoughts in an upheaval, her pride in shreds. What irony! She had been offered the kind of marriage that she had professed to want to the only man that she had the slightest interest in wedding, and she was miserably unhappy.

When the doctor emerged from her father's room, he warned her that she must spare him as much anxiety as possible. 'Agitation is very bad for him. I will not mince words with you, Lady Caroline. I fear that his incessant worrying about what will happen to you when he dies is having the unfortunate effect of hastening that day. He just told me that you have received a very flattering offer, and it is my frank opinion that if your father were to see you settled, it might be the best medicine that he could be given.'

Hearing that, no daughter who loved her father as much as Caro did could think of refusing the 'very flattering offer'. With a breaking heart, Caro resigned herself to a lifetime of unhappiness with a man who would never love her.

CHAPTER FOURTEEN

Taking leave of Dr Baxter, Caro would have fled to her room to indulge in a bout of weeping, but she was denied this melancholy release by the appearance of a servant with word that Lord Vinson awaited her in the morning-room.

Slowly she descended the stairs, feeling years older than she had when this day had begun.

As she entered the morning-room, her wayward heart leaped at the sight of her future husband, who looked so very handsome in a green double-breasted coat that accentuated the emerald of his eyes. His face was grave, as it had been when she had last seen him in the hall. She stopped inside the door, suddenly feeling awkward, shy and uncertain with him.

He came towards her, a strained little smile on his lips that she did not find reassuring. His green eyes were serious, almost sombre, as they regarded her. Did they reflect his displeasure at the thought of marrying such a plain creature as herself? Mindful of the gratitude she owed him for rescuing her from Tilford, she said a little stiffly, 'It was very kind of you to agree to marry me.' Her candour would not permit her to stop there. 'Although I own I cannot understand why you did.'

'I could not let you fall into Tilford's hands,' he said quietly.

His answer made her feel worse. Her voice cracked a little as she said, 'That is excessively kind of you, but I cannot see what you gain from your kindness.'

He gently took her small hands, oddly cold for so hot a day, into his own warm ones. His touch made her heart beat so hard against her ribs that she was certain he must be able to hear it.

'What I gain, elfin, is a wife.'

'But not one you could want, for I am not a lady or a great beauty, or even pretty. Surely you could find a more suitable bride?'

Alarm flashed in his eyes, and his hands released hers abruptly. 'If you are trying to tell me that you do not wish to marry me, elfin, you need only say so. My agreement to this match is conditioned upon its being acceptable to you. Is it?'

'Yes,' she admitted, wishing it were half so acceptable to him as it was to her.

Ashley was frowning. 'I am persuaded it is not. You look ready to cry.'

'My father is dying. Is that not reason enough to want to cry?' she asked, resorting to half truth to pacify him.

His frown deepened. 'You know that I have an . . .' Words suddenly seemed to fail the usually urbane Viscount, and he looked decidedly uncomfortable.

'An agreeable connection,' Caro supplied helpfully.

'Does that distress you?' he asked anxiously, searching her face with concerned eyes.

Fear and pride warred with candour, and for once the latter lost. With heroic effort, Caro managed an indifferent shrug, determined that Ashley should never know the truth. 'You are free to do as you please. I told you once that the only marriage I would consider is one like Lady Fraser's, and now I shall have it. I give you my solemn word that I shall not interfere, and I would never...'

'Yes, I know you would never break your word,' Ashley said impatiently. 'But are you certain that...'

'Very certain,' she cried emphatically, eager to put an end to this painful discussion.

Apparently this convinced him, for, taking her hands in his again, he squeezed them. 'I give my word to you as I did to your father, elfin, that I shall take very good care of you.' Seeing her expression of disbelief, he demanded, 'Why do you look at me like that?'

She said slowly, 'I have seen how husbands in loveless marriages treat their wives.'

'My God, elfin, you cannot think that I would abuse you!'

'But you do not love me.'

'No,' he admitted.

Caro felt as though her heart had been stabbed with a very long knife.

'Nor do you love me, elfin, but I think we can deal very well together.' He gave her hands another comforting squeeze. 'I know how distasteful marriage is to you, but I promise I shall be an easy husband, and you will never suffer ill-treatment at my hands. You will be far happier with me than with Tilford.'

Caro, swallowing hard, forced a smile to her unwilling lips.

'Now, I fear,' Ashley said with a teasing gleam in his eye, 'I am expected to drop on bended knee and formally beseech you for your hand, but I am persuaded that you would find me quite ridiculous. And

I dare not kiss you, for you have told me how repulsive that would be.'

Had Caro's sensibilities not been so overset, she would have comprehended that he was quizzing her. But taking his words seriously, she was deeply wounded, thinking them further confirmation that he had no romantic interest in her. Her cheeks burned with embarrassment as she stammered that his superior understanding gratified her.

She did not understand why her reply brought such a frown to his face or why he took his leave of her rather abruptly.

Caro and Ashley were married that evening at Levisham's bedside with only the Reverend Mr Laken and Dr Baxter present. Not surprising under the circumstances, the ceremony was brief, with none of the joy usually attendant upon such occasions.

Afterwards, Caro insisted on remaining with the Marquess, but he soon fell asleep. An hour later, Ashley appeared to insist that she come and dine with him.

When she protested that she would not leave her father, Ashley's handsome face assumed a look of exaggerated disappointment. 'You told me that you would never break your word to anyone, elfin, but now that I have bound myself for life to you, I find that it was all a hum. You are not a woman of your word.'

'You know that is not true!' Caro exclaimed.

'Do I?' he responded with an innocence that was belied by the teasing light in his eyes. 'Only an hour after you vowed to, among other things, *obey* me, you refuse to do so. And,' he added mournfully, 'it is such a very small request, too.'

Caro smiled in spite of herself and let him lead her away. Smiling mischievously at him, she said, 'I would know whether you will insist on my obedience to every little whim of yours, my lord husband?'

He gave her arm a reassuring squeeze. 'You will not find me a demanding spouse, child, except when your welfare is at stake. I intend to keep my word to take very good care of you.'

She was deeply moved by both his touch and the solicitude that she read in his eyes, but his calling her 'child' destroyed some of her pleasure. It rankled that he regarded her more as a daughter or little sister than a woman and his wife.

Ashley led her downstairs to the terrace where, at his instructions, a table for two had been laid. It was laden with covered dishes, a small bride's cake, roses from the garden, a candelabrum and a bottle of fine champagne.

When they were seated, Ashley dismissed the footman who was waiting to serve them, saying he would do so himself. When the minion was gone, the Viscount gave an audible sigh of relief. 'At last!'

He gave her an irresistible smile, its warmth melting the edges of the cold depression that had gripped her since she had learned her father had been stricken.

'How difficult it is to be private with my bride.'

My bride. The words thrilled Caro.

Ashley lifted the bottle of champagne. 'We have not yet toasted our wedding.' He poured her a glass, then one for himself. 'To us, elfin,' he said simply, his eyes serious, as his glass touched hers. 'May our life together be far happier than the circumstances under which we had to wed.'

She would drink to that, but what would make him happy—his undisturbed liaison with Lady Roxley—would break Caro's heart. She wanted more from Ashley than he was prepared to give.

Ashley turned his attention to the feast beneath the covered dishes that Levisham's French chef had created: poached turbot in lobster sauce, roast chicken with truffles, quenelles in puff pastry, duchess rolls, stuffed lettuce and Flemish-style carrots.

During dinner, Ashley did his utmost to erase the awkwardness she felt and to cheer her with a series of amusing anecdotes about his family and his mis-adventures while growing up. She would, he assured her, love her new mother-in-law, for she was a de-lightful creature who charmed everyone from the ir-ascible old Queen Charlotte down to the lowliest scullery-maid. His father was a prime one, too, but plain-spoken and a high stickler into the bargain. The Earl was a man who knew what was due his title and position, which might make him seem stern and un-bending to her initially. Listening to this description, Caro wondered anxiously what the Earl would think of her.

After dinner, she insisted on returning to her father's room even though Dr Baxter told her that there was no need for her to do so. Levisham was resting easily. But Caro would not be dissuaded. Concern for her father was not her only motive. She remembered all too vividly Tilford's advances, and she was uncertain and uneasy, indeed a little frightened, about what to expect of a husband, es-pecially one who did not love his wife. Although

Ashley was not at all like Tilford, Caro had not been able to erase entirely the fear and loathing that her cousin had created in her. So she sought refuge at Levisham's bedside.

To her surprise, her new husband did not object, but joined her there. They dared not talk for fear of waking the Marquess, but Ashley held her hand comfortingly. The champagne had made her very sleepy, as Ashley had intended it should. After an hour or so in the silent, darkened room, where the only sound was the ticking of the clock and the breathing of her father, Caro fell asleep in her chair.

When Ashley was certain that she was deeply asleep, he lifted her from the chair and laid her on a chaise near by. After tucking a light blanket around her in case the night should grow cooler, he took his leave, wondering wryly whether any man had ever spent an odder wedding night.

CHAPTER FIFTEEN

CARO was overjoyed by the recovery, so remarkable that it bordered on the miraculous, that her father made in the wake of her marriage, confirming in her mind Dr Baxter's assertion that it would be the best medicine that could be prescribed for him.

Her happiness was heightened by Ashley's attention to her. He was unfailingly understanding and considerate, cheering her with his humour and amiability. With her father improving so rapidly, she felt no guilt about spending more and more time with her husband. They went on long rides in the early morning. The harvest had begun in the oat fields, and sometimes they would stop to watch. Later, they would picnic by the stream or walk through the park. When it rained, they played billiards or read together in the library. If Caro had not known better, she would have thought herself cherished by him. But she knew better. *He does not want to marry you... He needs a wife to give him an heir.*

A fortnight after their wedding, Caro and Ashley were reclining in a sunny spot along the stream, not far from where a portion of its water was diverted to fill Bellhaven's pond. She told him of how they skated on the pond when it was frozen over in the winter.

'Do you like to skate, elfin?' Ashley asked. He was stretched out on the grassy bank, idly twirling in his fingers a sprig of tansy crowned with a cluster of delicate yellow-gold flowers. He wore no coat, and his ruffled shirt was open at the throat.

'Oh, yes!' Caro exclaimed. She was sitting beside him. The awkwardness and unease and anxiety that she had initially felt with him after their wedding had quickly faded. She could not wish for a more delightful companion. Yet, to her puzzlement, he remained only that, demanding not even so much as a kiss. For a man who had married only to obtain an heir, this omission seemed very peculiar to Caro. Clearly, he must find the prospect of making love to her so distasteful after Lady Roxley that he intended to postpone it as long as possible.

Initially, Caro had thought that she would welcome such neglect. But now, studying Ashley's finely sculpted mouth, kissing him did not seem the least unpleasant to her. Emily's words echoed in her mind: *I promise you that when you lose your heart to a man, you will like his kisses very much. Indeed . . . you will yearn for them.*

So that was what had happened to her, Caro thought unhappily. She had foolishly fallen in love with a husband whose heart belonged to his beautiful *chère amie.*

Ashley, staring at the tansy he was twirling in his hand, said abruptly, 'I must return to London soon. I have urgent business to attend to there.'

'What business?' Caro asked uneasily.

'Nothing that you need trouble your head about,' he replied evasively, his eyes still on the tansy's button-like flowers.

Caro, certain that his business was Lady Roxley, looked wretchedly miserable.

Ashley, misinterpreting the source of her unhappiness, said hastily, 'Do not worry, elfin. I will not insist that you come with me. But I think you would enjoy London.'

The prospect of leaving her father and the security of Bellhaven for a city where she knew no one frightened Caro. Even more disturbing to her was the knowledge that her husband's lovely mistress was there and that he would be in her arms.

'No, I do not want to go there,' Caro cried, a touch of desperation in her voice.

'Why not?'

She had given her word that she would never mention Lady Roxley to him, and now Caro tried to come up with some other plausible reason. She stammered, 'I will not be able to ride or ice-skate or enjoy the flowers or...'

'Or climb trees, elfin?' Ashley teased. 'I shall regard that as a profound blessing. But you can ride in Hyde Park and ice-skate on Rosamund Pond, and you shall not lack for flowers to enjoy at Bourn House.'

'I do not want to go! Please let us remain at Bellhaven? Have you not enjoyed yourself here?' she asked anxiously.

Ashley sighed. 'Yes, elfin, I have, but I cannot stay. I must return to London.'

Caro's spirits suffered another depressing blow when the Earl of Bourn arrived late that night at Bellhaven without advance warning. Ashley had dispatched a messenger informing his father of his marriage. Upon receiving it, the Earl had set out in haste without his Countess, a circumstance that in itself always put him in ill humour.

His disposition was not at all improved by the sight of his new daughter-in-law, when Ashley introduced them in Levisham's library amid the leather-bound volumes.

Caro sensed Bourn's instant disapproval of her. She had so wanted to win his approbation that his negative reaction to her had the effect of rendering her uncharacteristically shy and silent with him, thereby showing her to even greater disadvantage.

Levisham, who had retired early, had already been asleep when the Earl arrived, so Caro lacked her father's supporting presence. Even Ashley's practised urbanity could not entirely paper over the tension and awkward silences between the Earl and his new daughter-in-law. Caro seized on the first excuse she could find to flee from Bourn's presence.

After she left them, the Earl said to Ashley, 'I cannot believe that you have married such a plain, awkward little drab. Have you taken leave of your senses?'

'But, Papa, I only did your bidding,' Ashley replied in an unperturbed voice. 'It was you who insisted that I must marry immediately in order to produce an heir. You yourself selected Caro as a young lady worthy of bearing a future Earl of Bourn. Indeed, you said that she might prove to be your favourite candidate.'

'That was because I had never seen her! Her father misled me unconscionably, writing to me that she was much like her mama. Why, there is not a particle of resemblance to that beautiful, enchanting creature. Do not try to gammon me that you have fallen passionately in love with Caro. I know your taste for dazzling women too well.'

'No, I will not profess that. We have known each other too short a time, and Caro is not the type of girl to inspire violent passion. However, I have grown very fond of her.' He smiled soothingly at his father. 'She is the only one of the seven young ladies on your list that I had the smallest wish to marry.'

'Why?' the startled earl demanded.

Ashley smiled. 'She will never bore me.'

The forbidding frown suddenly vanished from the Earl's lined face. 'So that is the way it is,' he said, more to himself than to Ashley, then changed the subject abruptly. 'Your mama is anxious to meet your wife.'

'I am persuaded that they will deal famously together. Caro presently shows to disadvantage, but her defects are superficial. I believe that I can contrive, with the aid of Mama and a good maid, to turn her into a very striking, if not beautiful, young lady.'

'I do not believe in miracles,' the Earl said grumpily.

'Trust me, Papa. Caro will be a daughter-in-law you can be proud of.'

'How long do you remain at Bellhaven?'

Ashley frowned. He had intended to return to London a week ago, but he had been enjoying his time with Caro so much that he had postponed his departure. He could do so no longer, however. The problem of Henry, which had become more urgent with Ashley's marriage, must be dealt with quickly or Caro could be in grave danger.

To Caro's relief, Bourn stayed only that night at Bellhaven. Although he seemed friendlier to her when he took his leave, she could not be easy with him and was much relieved to have him gone.

But her relief was short-lived. No sooner had he left than her husband announced that he, too, was departing for London.

Bidding Caro goodbye, he said, 'Summon me at once if your father's condition worsens, and I will return immediately. However, I think it highly unlikely that it will,' he said in a sarcastic tone that puzzled her. 'When I get to London, I shall insert an announcement of our marriage in the *Gazette*. I must warn you, elfin, that there will be a great deal of talk about our hasty marriage and your remaining here at Bellhaven, but I shall do my best to shield you from it.'

'Thank you,' she mumbled, staring down at the floor in an effort to hide how miserable she was that he was leaving her for London and Lady Roxley.

His fingers gently held her chin, tilting it up so that he could look into her eyes. Smiling down at her, he asked softly, 'Will you miss me, elfin?'

'Yes,' she admitted, her gaze meeting his green eyes, which were regarding her with a quizzical light. Fearful of what her own eyes might reveal to him, she lowered them to his sensual mouth. Her heart seemed to cease beating as she wondered again what it would be like to be kissed by it.

As if reading her thoughts, his fingertips lightly brushed her cheeks and his lips descended on hers in a kiss so tender that it made her ache. She hoped it would never end. But, far too soon, he lifted his mouth. She saw in his eyes an odd, speculative look that greatly puzzled her.

His voice was suddenly husky, 'Goodbye, elfin.'

Then he was gone—to Lady Roxley's arms. What other urgent business could have drawn him to London? Caro thought bitterly. He could not wait to return to his mistress.

CHAPTER SIXTEEN

IT WOULD have astonished Caro to learn that Ashley was looking forward to seeing Lady Roxley with trepidation, not eagerness.

He had not confided to her his father's insistence that he wed. Her hatred of Bourn for having prevented her from marrying his son had intensified over the years until Ashley was reluctant to mention his father's name in Estelle's presence. So she had had no notion that his real reason for going to Bellhaven was to look over a prospective wife.

He had bid her farewell as a bachelor, with no hint that this status might soon change. Indeed, he himself had had not the slightest suspicion that he would return a married man. He desperately wished that he could have had the opportunity to break the news to her before the knot had been tied, but he had not, thanks to Levisham's insistence on an immediate wedding.

Ashley's lips compressed as he thought of the Marquess's amazing 'recovery'. The Viscount was growing increasingly certain that he had been gulled into a marriage that he had not wanted. But, oddly enough, he did not feel bitter about it. He would not have married Caro otherwise, but now that he had, he was not displeased with the match. He did, however, resent Levisham's insistence on keeping his daughter with him and his causing her so much needless anxiety with his feigned attack. In retaliation, Ashley had considered demanding that Caro return to London with him, but he had abandoned that notion because it would only have caused her more unhappiness.

Vinson had delayed publication of the notice about their marriage until he could break the news to Estelle in person. Although he dreaded this task, at the very least he owed her that courtesy rather than writing to her of it or, worse, having her see the advertisement in the *Gazette*. On reaching London, he resolved to see her as quickly as possible and get the unpleasant task over with.

He knew that Estelle would be angry and displeased by his marriage, even though she was the one who had rejected his offer in favour of her husband's. But Ashley thought that she would come round quickly. After all, she belonged to a society whose members often had to marry for reasons other than love and was herself a sophisticated woman of easy virtue. It had been she who had initiated their present affair, and, although she pretended otherwise, Ashley was certain that there had been other lovers before him.

He sent a note asking her to meet him that afternoon at the home of her bosom bow, Lady Brush. The lovers met there frequently under the guise of calling on her ladyship. Once both had arrived, their understanding hostess would obligingly disappear, leaving them alone for a happy interlude.

Ashley decided to visit Henry Neel while he was waiting for Estelle's answer. The Viscount had always been friendly with his cousin, the only member of the Neel family who was. Before Ashley went in search of the one-eared man, he wanted to give Henry a chance to rebut the evidence against him. The Viscount sincerely hoped that Henry could offer a less sinister explanation for his actions.

Vinson discovered that his cousin had recently moved from his modest rented rooms to a far more fashionable house in Chesterfield Street, where Henry received him in the drawing-room. He was a muscular man with hard grey eyes that revealed nothing. Ashley suspected that those eyes were his cousin's chief asset at the gaming-tables. He looked every one of his forty years, but his face was still handsome despite the dissipated lines that were becoming more pronounced. His habitual cynical expression gave way briefly to astonishment at the sight of his cousin, and he enquired sarcastically, 'What momentous reason has prompted your illustrious lordship to call on your poor relation?'

'Come now, Henry,' Ashley chided gently. 'Have I ever been so high in the instep as to deserve that greeting?'

'No,' his cousin agreed. 'That was churlish of me. You were never like that pompous brother of yours.'

Ashley stiffened imperceptibly at this contemptuous reference, although he would be the first to admit that Henry had reason for bitterness. William had made it abundantly—and very publicly—clear that he considered his cousin too far beneath his touch to notice.

'What do you think of my new home?' Henry asked.

Ashley looked about the expensively furnished room. 'An elegant house at an elegant address. You must be doing well at the tables.'

'It has been some years since I was under the hatches, and I do not expect to be there again.'

Ashley wondered whether that was because Henry also anticipated inheriting the Bourn fortune. 'What prompted you to take a house?'

'I desire respectability. The Neel family will have to find another black sheep to look down its collective nose at.' Seeing Ashley's startled look, he said bitterly, 'No, don't deny that's the way they feel about me. You were the only one who was even civil to me.'

'Merely civil?'

Henry smiled. 'No, a good deal more than that. I haven't forgotten how you helped me out from time to time when my pockets were all to let. You took quite a risk doing so. If that sanctimonious brother of yours had ever learned of your loans to me, he would have insisted your father cut off your funds. I often wondered why you bothered with me.'

'I liked you.' And that was the truth. Henry never pretended to be more or better than he was, making no excuses for himself, his gambling, or his exploits in the petticoat line. He was as apt to turn his mocking sense of humour against himself as anyone else.

'Liked me, did you?' Henry snorted. 'To be sure, you were the only Neel that ever did. That puffed-up brother of yours made it very plain that I was an embarrassment to the exalted family name.'

'I never thought you cared a whit what William thought,' Ashley said in surprise.

'I would not have given him that satisfaction,' Henry retorted bitterly.

Ashley felt suddenly chilled. 'You hated William, didn't you?'

'Detested him,' Henry replied bluntly. 'I don't adhere to that rubbish about not speaking ill of the dead.'

'Did you detest him enough to murder him?' Ashley asked with equal bluntness.

The colour faded from Henry's face. 'What?' he demanded hoarsely.

'Did you kill my brother?'

Henry winced. For a fraction of a second, his eyes broke contact with Ashley's, betraying him.

The Viscount stared at his cousin in shocked disbelief. 'Good God, Henry!'

Recovering himself, his cousin said, 'I did not murder William!'

For a moment, the room was as silent as a tomb as the two men's gazes locked. Henry looked away first, saying sharply, 'You have no evidence against me.'

'What about the one-eared man that Mercer Corte saw sneaking from the stable the night before the race?'

Henry shrugged. 'What about him?'

'Who is he?'

'How should I know?'

'Are you in the habit of meeting with men you do not know in the back slums of the Holy Land?'

His cousin glared at him in sullen silence.

'Why, Henry? Is it the title that you want?'

'I told you, I did not murder William!'

'You don't know how much I wish I could believe you.'

'No, I don't!' Henry said bitterly. 'You cannot wait to convict the family's black sheep unjustly on the flimsiest of evidence. And I thought you were different from the others.'

'And I thought you were better,' Ashley said, his disillusionment echoing in his voice.

'What do you mean to do now?'

Ashley rose. 'Expose the truth. If you were responsible for William's death, I swear to you that I shall see you in Newgate.'

He turned on his heel and went to the door.

Henry called after him, his voice as ominous as a sudden thunderclap, 'I warn you, Vinson, leave well enough alone, or you will regret it!'

CHAPTER SEVENTEEN

WHEN Ashley returned to Bourn House from his visit to Henry, Estelle's frigid reply to his note awaited him. If he wished to see her, he could call on her at her home in Hertford Street. Both the tone of her message and the location she had chosen for their meeting told him that he was in her black books even before she learned of his marriage.

Riding to Hertford Street, it occured to Ashley that not only was he dreading this meeting with Estelle, but that he had not missed her nearly so much as he had expected to during his absence at Bellhaven.

Lady Roxley received him in her drawing-room. After her note, he was not surprised that her greeting was as cold and formal as the room itself, with its stiffly arranged furniture. She remained seated on a Sheraton settee that was placed against the far wall, forcing him to cross the room to her.

As he did, he observed, as he had so often, what a jewel of rare loveliness she was. Indeed, he always thought of her in terms of gems: her eyes were a unique and startling violet that reminded him of a pair of flawless amethysts; her lips were ruby red against a complexion as creamy and lustrous as fine pearls; her raven hair shone like jet. Legions of besotted admirers had likened her to Aphrodite.

She did not rise to greet Ashley and extended no invitation for him to sit. He remained standing before her while she eyed him coldly, making clear her displeasure with him. At last she silently offered him a slender hand, its fingers weighted with costly rings. As he brought it to his lips, she petulantly demanded why he had been so tardy in returning to London—and to her.

'I fear that being my father's heir entails certain onerous duties,' he said with a rueful sigh, 'one of which I was obliged to discharge.'

Only slightly mollified, she asked coolly, 'What was this time-consuming obligation?'

'Marriage.'

A startled gasp escaped her lips. 'I do not find such a joke amusing!'

'I do not joke. I have married Levisham's daughter. But it need have no effect on our connection,' Ashley hastened to reassure her. 'Duty need not interfere with pleas—'

A torrent of fury, more ungenteel than anything Ashley had heard even from the most inelegant of the muslin company, erupted from Estelle's beautiful ruby lips like a volcanic eruption.

It was several moments before she regained sufficient control of herself and her tongue to realise that her lover had dropped her hand and was staring at her in appalled silence. Recognising her error, she gave him a beseeching look, asking in broken-hearted accents how he could have betrayed her love for him so cruelly by marrying another.

'Why are you so distressed that I have acquired a wife when it was you who foreclosed the possibility of our marrying by spurning my offer and wedding another man?' he asked her, not unreasonably.

When Bourn had said he would cut his younger son off without a penny should he marry her, Estelle had preferred to be rich Lady Roxley to penniless Mrs Neel. But she had been far too clever to tell Ashley that. Instead, she had assured him that although she loved him wildly, she could not bear to be the cause of an estrangement between him and the Earl, thereby cunningly assuring the very break between father and son that she had professed to want to avoid.

Now, she wanted to scream at Ashley that she had rejected him when he had been a second son who appeared to have no chance to inherit the Bourn title or fortune, but she could not tell him that. Instead, she asked in her most wounded tone, 'How can you treat me so cruelly when I love you so?'

The Viscount's eyebrow rose. 'Yes, you loved me so much that you married Roxley instead,' he said drily.

'Surely you are not jealous of him? You have no reason to be.'

'No,' he agreed amiably, 'I do not.'

She stared at him uneasily, uncertain of how to interpret his answer.

'You know that I must marry for an heir,' Ashley said softly.

Estelle, who had hoped to be the mother of that heir, felt as though she would choke on her own frustration. She had been certain that her boring, clutch-fisted husband, twenty years her senior, would meet the early demise he deserved, freeing her to marry Ashley and become the Countess of Bourn. 'Roxley will not live for ever,' she snapped.

'Neither will I,' Ashley retorted coolly.

His unexpected attitude worried Estelle, and abruptly she switched tactics. Burying her face in her handkerchief, she cried, 'You have broken my heart.

You are the only man that I have ever loved, and now you have played me false. Marrying behind my back without even a word to me. Go away, you heartless creature.'

'Estelle,' he began, putting his arm about her shoulder. 'Pray, do not...'

But she jerked away from him, crying dramatically. 'Go away at once! I cannot bear the sight of your perfidious face!'

To her astonishment, instead of pleading with her to let him stay, he rose, saying abruptly, 'As you wish.'

Estelle watched him move towards the door of the drawing-room, certain that he was expecting her to stop him. But she would not. Instead, she would let him worry that he had lost her. She would bring him to his knees, and he would pay a handsome price to be restored to her good graces—and to her boudoir. She would see to that.

Already she could envision the ruby and diamond necklace that she had admired last week at her favourite jeweller encircling her swan-like neck.

Caro had known that she would miss Ashley, but she was unprepared for how much. Unprepared, too, for how lonely she was without him. She had become shockingly accustomed to his cosseting of her, and she missed spending her days with him. Touching her lips, she remembered his kiss and yearned for more. How right Emily had been.

Three days after Ashley's departure, a discreet announcement of their marriage was published in the *Gazette*. Its appearance was followed the next day by the arrival of Olive Kelsie at Bellhaven. The newspaper notice had wiped out in one stroke her two most cherished dreams, and she had set out posthaste for Bellhaven to assure herself that the announcement was a malicious, libellous error.

Remembering the Marquess's ban on her appearance there, she asked to see Caro, telling the butler, 'Do not bother the Marquess. My business is only with his daughter.'

The servant nodded enigmatically. He had no intention of sending the Marquess into a pelter.

When Caro confirmed to Olive that she and Ashley were married, her aunt could not contain her rage and venom. 'No doubt you think yourself quite the thing to have hooked such a prime catch, but you are a prime fool!' Olive's eyes glittered malevolently. 'He has a mistress with whom he is wildly in love.'

'Yes, I know,' Caro replied with her characteristic honesty.

The answer deflated her aunt momentarily, but she recovered quickly. 'He married only because his father ordered it. I myself heard Vinson proclaim that it did not matter in the slightest to him whom he married because he could not wed the woman he loved. With my own ears, I heard him say that he would happily accept any woman who would turn a blind eye to sharing him with his mistress.'

Her aunt's words stabbed Caro like a rapier-blade. So that was why her father had been so emphatic that she give Ashley her word she would not object to his mistress. Caro recalled again with burning clarity Ashley's answer when she had asked him the day they met why he was not married: I have known no lady as complaisant as you.

'My own daughters refused to accept him on such insulting terms,' Olive continued, ignoring the fact

that, despite her best efforts, neither of her daughters
was given a chance to do so. 'Have you not a shred
of pride that you would agree to such a demeaning
bargain? No, of course you do not.' She laughed contemptuously. 'Such an antidote as you cannot afford
pride. You were far too happy to catch a man to care
what the terms might be.'

But Caro had a great deal of pride; too much to
let her aunt know how devastated she was by her
revelations.

'Where is your bridegroom?' Olive demanded.

When Caro told her, Olive jeered, 'So, after less
than a fortnight of marriage, he has fled from you
for London and Lady Roxley! No doubt you think
that in time you can lure him away from her. What
a fool you are! She is the most beautiful woman in
England, and he has been mad for her for years. You
will never take Vinson away from her.'

'I do not care,' Caro said with as much dignity as
she could muster in her pain. She was determined not
to let her aunt know how very much she did care, and
her chin tilted proudly. 'I have always said that the
only marriage I would consider was one like Lady
Fraser's, and now I have it.' Yes, she did, God help
her!

'If you are such a fool, your father is not. What
could he have been thinking of to permit such a humiliating union?'

Humiliating union! Her aunt's cruel words goaded
Caro into replying, 'He felt, as I do, that *anything*
was preferable to being forced to marry your odious
son.'

Olive was speechless at the revelation that Levisham
had divined her ambition and outwitted her just when

it seemed within her grasp. Then her rage overcame her, and she screamed, 'You impertinent chit! I promise you that you'll rue the day you made such a devil's bargain with Vinson.'

CHAPTER EIGHTEEN

Two weeks later, Levisham and Caro were sitting on the terrace at Bellhaven when Abigail Foster was announced.

'Here!' Caro cried in surprise, delighted that Abigail, whom she loved like an older sister, had returned for a visit. 'I had no notion she was not in Scotland.'

When Abigail appeared in the doorway to the terrace, Caro exclaimed, 'What a wonderful surprise, isn't it, Papa?'

But he did not seem to share her delight. His face had hardened, and he said nothing.

'Your sister-in-law said nothing about your coming for a visit! When did you...' Caro's voice trailed off in shock as Abigail stepped out of the shadow of the doorway into the full light of the terrace.

Her habitual vivacious demeanour was nowhere in evidence. Her pretty face looked worn, weary, and years older than when she had left for Scotland a mere nine months before. She leaned on her long, unfashionable umbrella as if for support. Her gown was old, unbecoming, and travel-worn. Her sky-blue eyes no longer sparkled but were dull and sad, and now they looked apprehensively at Levisham, as though uneasy about the welcome he would accord her.

'Neither my sister-in-law nor my brother has the smallest notion that I am here, and I pray that you will not tell them.' Abigail turned an entreating face toward Levisham. She gasped as she took in his shrunken body and wan, hollow-eyed face. An agonised look contorted her own features.

Caro, who thought her father's improvement in recent days amazing, was startled by their guest's reaction. Then she remembered that Abigail had left for Scotland before the fever that so decimated Levisham had struck him last spring, and had not seen him since.

'Oh, God, George,' Abigail burst out, 'what is wrong? You look so very ill!'

She looked as though she wanted to throw herself into the invalid's arms. In that unguarded moment, Caro saw in Abigail's eyes the same unconsciously speaking look that Emily often gave Mercer Corte. *Abigail was in love with her father!*

Turning to him, Caro saw the harsh, angry expression that he had worn since Abigail's arrival suddenly soften.

'Although I may not look it, I am much improved,' he said.

'I don't understand.' Abigail's confused voice again betrayed the depth of her feelings. 'You have always been the strongest man I know.'

'One would almost think you cared,' the Marquess said bitterly.

'I do care!' she exclaimed violently. Belatedly realising what she was revealing, she amended hastily, 'You have always been a most cherished friend of my father and myself.'

'Have I now?' Levisham responded wryly, an odd light in his grey eyes. 'Why are you here when you do not want your brother and his wife to know that you are in the neighbourhood?'

A dull red flush spread over Abigail's face and she stared down at her feet. 'I have run away from my aunt. She is such a dour, evil-tempered old harridan, complaining endlessly about everything and everyone, that I would rather die than remain in her company! I was nothing but her unpaid servant without a moment's respite from her ceaseless demands.'

Levisham studied Abigail's dusty, travel-wrinkled costume. 'What do you propose to do now?'

She lifted her eyes, brimming with sadness, and looked out across the formal garden that lay below the terrace. 'I cannot go to my brother, for his odious wife will insist that I be returned to my aunt. And I have no money, for although Papa left me a respectable income, he placed it under my brother's control. Darrow is as clutch-fisted as Amelia Coleberd's husband, and, like Amelia, I have no recourse. It is not fair!'

'Life rarely is,' Levisham said coldly.

Abigail cast a beseeching look at him. 'I know that you no doubt wish me at Jericho and that I have no right to make such a request of your generosity, but there is no one else I can apply to. I was hoping that you might see fit to hire me as a companion-chaperon for Caro until she marries.'

'She is already married.'

'What?' Abigail's startled eyes flew first to Levisham's face, then to Caro's. 'Surely you cannot be!' Her proudly straight shoulders collapsed in despair.

Caro, her soft heart wrung by her friend's dejection, hurried to her side and put her arms about her.

'Who is your husband?' Abigail asked.

'Lord Vinson,' Levisham interposed.

Abigail's eyes widened in amazement. 'You jest!'

'Why should you think so?' Levisham demanded coldly.

Poor Abigail, blushing scarlet, stammered, 'Caro is not at all in Vinson's usual style.'

Caro hid the pain that Abigail's words caused her. Even her dear friend recognised what a mésalliance her marriage was. But Caro had no time to waste on her own unhappiness in the face of Abigail's. Tightening her arms round the older woman, Caro assured her, 'I should like very much to have you as my companion.'

'Put that notion from your mind, Caro,' Levisham said curtly.

Tears welled in Abigail's eyes, and she whispered mournfully, 'I do not know what I shall do.'

Caro, feeling her own eyes grow moist in sympathy, cried, 'Papa, how can you be so cruel, turning her away like this?'

'I am not turning her away. She may stay here as long as she wishes.'

Abigail's startled gaze flew up to meet Levisham's. 'But I cannot. My brother, when he learns that I am here, will never permit me to intrude on your hospitality, unless I have a legitimate occupation to earn my keep. Nor,'—her head raised proudly—'would I want to.'

The Marquess gave her a long searching look. 'I wish to be private with Abigail,' he told Caro sharply.

Puzzled, Caro rose and went to the French doors that led into the drawing-room.

'Shut the doors behind you,' her father instructed her, 'and see that we are not disturbed by anyone.'

When the doors had closed behind his daughter, Levisham gestured towards the chair beside him which she had vacated. 'Sit there, Abigail.'

Reluctantly his visitor, casting a nervous glance at him from beneath her lashes, did as she was bid.

He was torn between happiness at seeing her again and a fresh surge of anger at her rejection of the offer he had made her after his son's death. Despite her having turned down several attractive proposals and her oft-stated determination not to marry and place herself under a husband's uncertain domination, Levisham had thought that his own suit would meet with a warmer reception. When it had not, his consequence had been bitterly wounded. More surprisingly, so had his heart. Somehow, over the years, without his realising it, Abigail had come to occupy a very important place in his affection and in his life. But it had taken her departure to Scotland for him to acknowledge this belatedly to himself.

Abigail was toying nervously with the handle of her umbrella, and said, 'I am shocked that Caro has married Lord Vinson.'

'Why should you be? They are well matched in birth and family.'

'Does the heart count for nothing?' Abigail asked softly, her eyes meeting his shyly. 'Vinson loves his mistress, who is an incomparable beauty. Why would he suddenly want to marry Caro?'

'He did not. His father insisted that he must marry. The Earl wants a grandson.'

'Oh, George,' Abigail cried, her hands closing convulsively round the handle of her umbrella. 'How could you marry your daughter to a man who wants nothing but to have her bear his child? What kind of life will she have?'

'Vinson is an honourable man.' Levisham would not confess his own misgivings about the match he had arranged. Instead, he said defensively, 'I believe that he will treat Caro always with great kindness and consideration.'

'Will kindness and consideration be enough for Caro?' Abigail demanded angrily, a haunted look in her eyes. 'What of love?'

The Marquess glared at her. How dared she question him when, to his thinking, she was as much responsible for his daughter's marriage as he was. If only Abigail had accepted his offer. She was as sensible a woman as he had ever known (except for her one unaccountable lapse in refusing his suit), and he could have trusted her to protect both his daughter and her fortune. He would have been able to leave Caro in her stepmother's custody rather than requiring her to make a marriage she did not want. Furthermore, by now he might have fathered another son, who would have kept the odious Tilford from the succession.

Although Levisham was not normally a vindictive man, he could not restrain himself, in the face of these unhappy thoughts, from telling Abigail, 'You were a fool not to have accepted my offer. Had you married me, you would not be in this miserable situation.'

Her head snapped up and for a moment there was a flash of her old spirit in her eyes. 'Nor would I be in it had you not made me that wretched offer!'

'What are you talking about?' he demanded.

'My father was so incensed over my refusing you that he altered his will to punish me, denying me control of my inheritance. He knew how important it was to me to be independent. Furthermore, I think it was your dreadful sister-in-law who gave Darrow's wife the idea that she would be well rid of me.'

Knowing Olive as he did, Levisham did not doubt that Abigail's suspicion was well founded. 'Damn that woman!'

'That would do me little good now,' Abigail retorted with a hint of her old humour.

Levisham studied her for a long moment, considering the question that had plagued him since she had rejected his proposal. Until now, his pride had prevented him from asking it. 'Let us be honest with each other, Abigail. You told me a few minutes ago that you cared about me. Why then did you so blithely refuse my offer?'

'I did not blithely refuse your offer, but if you were to ask me again today, I would still reject it.'

'I do not understand. You said you cared.'

Her blue eyes met his squarely. 'I do care,' she said quietly. 'I have been in love with you since I was Caro's age.'

He gaped at her, his emotions fluctuating wildly between happiness and bewilderment. 'Then why did you refuse me?'

'Because you do not love me. You never showed me the least interest during all those years until Brandon died. Then you offered for me only because you wanted an heir to prevent Tilford from inheriting.'

He squirmed at the truth of her charge. Yes, that had been the reason he had offered for her. She was a pleasant, witty companion, and he had thought that they would deal well together. Over the years, he had become so used to having her about that he had rarely given her a second thought. Occasionally it had crossed his mind that she would make an excellent wife and mother for his children, but, if the truth be known, he hated London and much preferred the reclusive life that he had led since his wife's death. Were he to remarry, he would no longer be able to use the excuse of extended grief over her death. Both society and a new wife would expect him to re-enter the fashionable world. It had taken the ramifications of his son's death to end his lassitude.

Abigail regarded him sombrely. 'I could not live my life with a husband who would always love the memory of another woman instead of me,' she said with a dignity that wrenched his heart.

For the first time, he comprehended how insulting his offer must have seemed to her. He had not presented it in romantic terms because he had not yet realised himself how much he loved her. He passed a hand over his face. How many mistakes he had made. Only now, when his future was so uncertain, was he aware of them. He prayed that he would be permitted to live long enough to try to make up to Abigail for some of the pain and hurt he had caused her.

His hands reached out and caught hers. 'My dearest Abigail, what an incredible fool I have been. I do love you very much, but it took me a long time to realise it. I would like to make you another offer, but I must warn you that you run the risk of being a widow almost before you are a wife.'

'Oh, George, that does not matter.' Tears welled up in her eyes. 'To have you and your love for a little while would be so much better than never to have had it.'

*   *   *

A servant told Caro that her father wished to see her on the terrace. She hurried out to find Abigail and the Marquess holding hands. When they told her that they planned to be married, Caro was delighted. 'It is the very best thing for both of you!' she exclaimed exuberantly.

Later, when she was alone with Abigail, she asked with her customary frankness, 'How long have you been in love with Papa?'

'For years, but he was so wrapped up in his memories of your mama that he scarcely noticed my existence.' Abigail's smile faded. 'I felt that I could never compete with her memory. But I was determined to marry no one but him. My father would never have permitted my remaining single for that reason. So I pretended to embrace Lady Fraser's disgust for marriage. I insisted that I wished to devote myself to caring for Papa. Since his paramount concern was for his own comfort, which I saw to nicely, he was delighted for me to remain at his side.'

'Your father did not deserve you!' Caro cried.

Abigail shrugged. 'It suited me to remain with him because it permitted me to be near your papa.'

Caro was appalled by what her friend had silently suffered for all those years: hiding her love for a man who did not return it while tending to a demanding old tyrant. 'How unhappy you must have been.'

'But no longer!' Happiness radiated from Abigail's face, but suddenly it vanished like the sun behind a black cloud, and she cried in a choked voice, 'Oh, Caro, your father looks so weak. I could not bear to lose him now. I love him so!'

Caro's heart ached for her friend. If only her father had made Abigail an offer years ago, instead of wasting all those years when they might have been happy together.

When Caro expressed this sentiment aloud, Abigail replied in a voice laced with sorrow, 'But he had to discover first that he loved me. Living with him without his love would have been too painful for me to bear. Oh, Caro, you have no idea how terrible it is to know that the man you love adores another, far more dazzling, woman!'

But Caro did know. Even now, Ashley was no doubt in the arms of Lady Roxley. The thought twisted in Caro like a medieval torture-screw.

CHAPTER NINETEEN

SEVERAL days had passed since Ashley had called on Lady Roxley to tell her of his marriage, and she had not heard from him. Visions of the ruby and diamond necklace gave way to alarm in the lady's mind. She had expected to be showered with flowers and trinkets and beseeching notes pleading for forgiveness. But she had heard not a word.

Estelle, recalling the universal admiration still accorded the late, legendary Marchioness of Levisham, wondered anxiously whether the daughter could be an Incomparable like her mother.

It had not occurred to Lady Roxley initially that Ashley's wife might have his heart, because Estelle could not conceive that any man so sublimely fortunate as to be her lover could possibly notice another woman. Furthermore, Vinson had referred to his marriage as an onerous duty and assured her that his marriage 'need have no effect on our connection'.

Despite Estelle's pique at Ashley's marriage, she did not want to lose him. She had had other lovers before him, and none had been so satisfying, or so generous and entertaining, as Vinson. Years ago, when he had first fallen in love with her, she had wrapped him about her finger. But in the intervening years, he had changed, and for all the devotion he showed her, she was no longer so certain of her power over him. How she wished now that she had married him so that he would be legally tied to her for life.

She remembered uneasily the way that he had looked at her after she lost her temper at the news of his marriage. If only she had not done so. Her servants, her children and the rest of her family lived in terror of her temper, but she had always taken great care never to let Ashley see that unattractive side of her. Accustomed as she was, however, to unswerving male adoration, Ashley's taking of a wife had been more than her pride could bear. She had been humiliated by the thought that everyone would talk about his defection from her.

But after the first shock of his news had worn off, she realised that she could squelch such unflattering gossip by showing London that, despite his new wife, he was still hers. This task would be made easier by his not having brought his wife to London with him, an omission that was causing considerable speculation.

Going to her rosewood-and-gilt writing-table, Estelle penned a note to Ashley, bidding him to come to her house at noon the following day. They could not meet at the Brushes'. Lady Brush had been so lacking in foresight as to invite two dozen ladies of the ton there to hear Lord Byron read his poetry at the very time that Estelle wished to rendezvous with Ashley. He would not come to her house, however, if he knew that her husband was in town, so she refrained from informing him that this was the case.

Even though Roxley was in town, his lady knew that she would run no danger of his discovering her with Ashley. Her husband spent his afternoons at his club, dining there before going on to whatever entertainments he had scheduled for the night. Estelle could not remember when he had last been home in the afternoon or when they had dined there together.

She sent her invitation to Ashley by hand. The footman returned with a reply that the Viscount could not come at noon but would do so at four.

This vexed Estelle greatly, for she had planned to greet him in her dressing-room. Despite this pedestrian designation, it was an elegant chamber. Its walls, which were hung with crimson and gold brocade, provided a flattering backdrop for her dramatic beauty. An alcove with a day-bed in it occupied one end of the room. Crimson and gold draperies, which matched the wall hangings, could be drawn across the alcove's arched opening to ensure privacy.

It was on the day-bed that Estelle had planned to greet Ashley, clad in her most provocative négligée, and to proceed to strengthen her hold over him with an afternoon of delightful improprieties in that cleverly curtained alcove. But although a négligée would seem unexceptional at noon, since that was the hour at which she normally rose, still to be wearing it at four in the afternoon would too blatantly broadcast her intent.

So, the following afternoon, she was forced instead to don a new silk gown with a fitted waist, from which a full skirt billowed over several petticoats. In truth, it would have been more appropriate for an assembly at Almack's than an afternoon in her dressing-room, but she believed it was the most flattering gown she owned. The intense shade of rose enhanced the pearl-like lustre of her complexion; the fitted waist emphasised her own, which was amazingly tiny for a woman who had borne three sons; and the gown's daring décolletage revealed two of her best assets.

She was determined to be her most charming when Ashley arrived, even though her husband had put her dreadfully out of curl that morning by announcing that he was having their sons brought to London from their country house in Dorset. They would arrive that night, and he would spend it at home so that he would be there when they came.

It was just like that disobliging man to come home early on the one day when she wanted him out of the house for as long as possible. Estelle had never loved him, but when they were first married, he had adored her and had been only too happy to give her whatever she wanted.

But as the years passed, he had grown increasingly irate over her extravagances until, after the birth of their third son, he had humiliated her by cutting off her generous allowance, making it known to the fashionable shopkeepers she patronised that they could expect no payment unless he had first approved her expenditures. None of her teasing and cajoling, or even her extravagant temper tantrums, had made him relent. Since she had married him only for his fortune and he was withdrawing its free use, she saw no reason why she should be his wife in anything but name, and she made it clear that the less she saw of him, the better.

To her surprise, he had accepted her edict without argument. It never occurred to her that he might have come to feel the same way.

When Ashley arrived, she received him in her dressing-room. Skirts swaying gracefully, she moved to greet him with a seductive smile. He looked so dashing in his elegant frock coat of dark blue superfine over a striped blue waistcoat and a frilled white shirt.

Seeing her, he stopped. 'How beautiful you are!'

This remark made her feel more confident of him. Extending her hands to him, she said in her most provocative voice, low and husky and enticing, 'It has been days since I have seen you. I hope this is not how you mean to neglect me now that you are married?'

He took her hands and kissed first one, then the other. 'You told me at our last meeting that you could not bear the sight of me.'

'You must understand the terrible shock you gave me: the love of my life marrying without so much as a word of warning in advance.' She continued to hold his hands, and her husky voice became softly chiding. 'If only you had told me before you left how you felt about Levisham's daughter.'

'I could not do that then, for I had not yet met her myself.'

Thoroughly alarmed by this answer, Estelle demanded, a hint of incredulity in her tone, 'Are you saying that it was love at first sight?'

Her question seemed to amuse Ashley greatly. 'No, it was not.'

Although relieved, Estelle continued to probe. 'If it was not love, why did you marry her so quickly?'

'For several reasons, but love was not one of them.'

'No doubt she fell into your arms the moment she saw you,' Estelle said tartly.

'As a matter of fact, she did,' Ashley replied, his lips twitching.

Estelle, knowing how much he disliked aggressive young ladies, was delighted that his wife should have been so stupidly forward in her pursuit of him.

Leading Ashley towards the alcove, Estelle cooed, 'Oh, darling, I wish that you could have come at noon. Our time together shall have to be short.'

'Why?' he asked with a frown.

'Roxley is having the children brought to London, and they arrive tonight.'

Ashley's frown vanished. 'I understand. Of course, you wish to be with your children.'

'It's not that at all,' she said, looking at him as though he were touched in the upper works. Motherhood had been as disappointing to her as marriage. She had detested pregnancy, with its morning sickness and the awkwardness and discomfort of growing huge, not to mention her intense fear of dying in childbirth. Then came the agony of birth—and all for wrinkled, red little brats so ugly that she could scarcely believe that they could have come from her exquisite body. Perhaps if they had been little girls, who could be dressed up charmingly in lace and frills like the dolls she used to play with, she might have found them more interesting. But sons were miniature whirlwinds always getting into things they should not. 'I infinitely prefer your company to that of my sons. But Roxley dotes on his boys, and he intends to return home by six so that he will be here when they arrive.'

'Good God, I thought he was out of town! I should not be here.' He looked about her dressing-room with an angry frown. 'I would not have come up had I known . . .'

Estelle silenced him by the simple expedient of covering his mouth with her own in a passionate kiss.

A knock at the door caused Ashley to set her firmly away from him.

'Do not disturb me,' Estelle called crossly in the direction of the door.

'Begging your pardon, milady, but your children are here,' said the butler, whom she was certain Roxley kept on solely to vex her, knowing how much she detested the old retainer. 'His lordship left word that if he had not yet returned when they arrived, they were to be brought to you.'

Estelle wanted to scream at him to take the brats away, but she dared not, for that meddling old fool would be certain to tell Roxley that she had done so because Ashley had been with her. Generally, her husband chose to ignore her infidelities, but he would cut up stiff if he learned that she had refused to see her children so that she could entertain her lover.

Her sons, aged four, five and six, filed into the room, looking like a flight of stairs. They eyed her nervously, stopping well back from her billowing gown. Nevertheless, she cautioned them against wrinkling her skirt. They were handsome children, having inherited her jet-black hair and their father's hazel eyes, but they were remarkably subdued for boys of their rumbunctious age who were seeing their mother for the first time in two months. Estelle, however, saw nothing odd about this, for she demanded such polite, well-mannered behaviour of them.

Her youngest, a thin, rather frail little boy, was clearly ill. His nose was red and running, his eyes, dull and feverish, and he looked perfectly miserable. She regarded him with a deep dismay that arose from concern for herself rather than for him. She had a profound fear of being exposed to any contagious illness, so certain was she that she herself would immediately contract it.

'Why must Justin always be ill?' she demanded petulantly of their nurse, a dragon-faced, middle-aged woman who had followed the children into the room.

'He's a sickly 'un, milady.' The woman's harsh tone proclaimed her contempt for such weakness.

'But, Mama, I cannot help it,' Justin protested mournfully in a voice so hoarse he could hardly be heard. 'I don't want to feel so awful.'

He took a step towards her, as if to seek solace, but she drew back in alarm, fearful for both her skirt and her health. 'It is time Nurse put you to bed.'

She ignored the two large tears that formed in his eyes, and said brightly, 'Now the three of you go with Nurse.'

'Yes, Mama,' they murmured in chorus, the older two looking as relieved to be going as she was to have them gone. As they turned towards the door, the eldest asked wistfully, 'When will Papa be home?'

'Soon,' she said curtly. Turning back to Ashley as the door closed behind her children, she gave an artificial little laugh. 'What nuisances children are. Always getting sick or in trouble. Come, darling.' She held out her hand to him, intending to lead him back to the alcove.

But he did not take it. Instead, he was studying her with the oddest look in his eyes. It was as though he were seeing her for the first time.

Finally, she said irritably, 'Come, we haven't much time.'

'No time at all,' he said, a peculiar note in his voice. 'I must leave. Your children arrived early; your husband may do so as well.'

'But,' she wailed, 'I...'

He cut her off, saying firmly, 'No, I must go.' He turned abruptly and was gone.

CHAPTER TWENTY

THREE DAYS after Abigail's arrival at Bellhaven, she and Levisham were married privately. Caro was overjoyed by the love that glowed with increasing intensity between her father and his bride. With Abigail to cosset him, his health showed such marked improvement that Dr Baxter remarked that the Marquess might surprise them all by living to a very old age.

With her father and Abigail lost in the private world of their love, Bellhaven seemed lonelier than ever to Caro without Ashley.

Each night, when Abigail and the Marquess retired to their bedchamber, Caro was reminded that although her husband had married her for an heir, he had taken no further step to attain that end. As happy as she was for the newlyweds, she could not help being a little sad, too, because it reminded her of how different her own strange marriage was.

Caro tried to ease her pain by reminding herself of how long it had taken for Abigail's unrequited love for Papa to be returned. But this thought offered her sorry comfort when she contemplated the many wasted years. A decade to a girl of seventeen was more than half a lifetime. In short, an eternity.

She thought of her husband constantly. Lonely and miserable without him, she was convinced that he was living happily in London with never a thought for the wife he had left behind.

Caro was wrong, however, on both counts. Ashley was far from happy. Despite his and Mercer Corte's diligent efforts to locate the one-eared man in the back slums of St Giles, they were unsuccessful. Without him, there would be no hope of building a case against Henry in William's death.

Meanwhile, Ashley's concern about his cousin's intentions had been heightened when, a week after his return to London, he had run into Henry at White's.

'It would be very wise of you, dear cousin,' Henry had told him, 'to cease your forays into St Giles, especially since they will gain you nothing.'

'Are you threatening me?' Ashley asked coldly.

'I believe it is felicitations on your marriage that are called for,' Henry replied blandly. 'Or are they? I understand that you have not seen fit to let London see your bride. She remains at Bellhaven with her father.'

Henry's pointed reference to Caro's whereabouts sharply increased Ashley's anxiety about her. He had thought that she would be safer at Bellhaven, but now he wished that she were at his side where he could keep his eye on her.

He redoubled his efforts to find the one-eared man, repeatedly visiting the alehouse where Mercer had seen him. Although he was certain that the individual he was seeking was well known to the tavern's habitués and proprietor, all professed to have not the slightest notion as to whom he could be. Even the generous reward Ashley offered failed to loosen their tongues. It quickly became clear that no one dared to betray the man he sought.

He and Mercer widened the search for information about the man, spending night after night in the Holy

Land, but his identity and whereabouts continued to elude them.

One night, after weeks of fruitless effort, they left a stinking sluicery, where the gin amply deserved its nickname of blue ruin, and turned down a crooked alley. There they were accosted by a runny-eyed, wheezing-voiced man dressed in shabby nankeen trousers and a coarse, much-mended shirt. He had clearly been waiting in the dark recesses of the alley for them to emerge from the sluicery.

Ashley had become sufficiently familiar with St Giles's Greek, as the slum's cant was called, to understand that the man was offering them information about their one-eared quarry for a price and on the condition that they never identity its source.

'It'll cost a score o' beans,' the stranger warned them. 'Oi ain't such a chub that Oi don't know ol' Chester would tuck me up with a spade if'n 'e found out. 'E don't miss with that barkin' iron of 'is, 'e don't.'

'Twenty guineas it will be if you tell me the rest of Chester's name and where I can find him,' Ashley agreed promptly.

The man responded in a torrent of St Giles's Greek that left Mercer staring at him blankly. Ashley, however, had understood him well enough to make out that Moking was the surname of the man they sought but that their informer did not know his present whereabouts. The wealthy man for whom Moking occasionally worked had paid him a large sum of money to disappear from London for a few months.

When Ashley asked for a description of Moking's benefactor, the informer gave one that fitted Henry, concluding admiringly, ''E's a well-breeched swell, 'e is. Gave old Chester a pile of rhino to go away, 'e did. Oi saw 'im 'and it o'er with me own eyes.' A shrewd look came into the man's watery eyes. 'Methinks the swell's afraid of riding the three-legged mare.'

After they left the man, Mercer remarked, 'I cannot fathom how a man could ride a three-legged mare or why he would want to.'

'Rest assured, he would not want to,' Ashley replied. 'It's the gallows. I wonder where Henry sent Moking.'

'What will you do now?'

'Continue to offer a large reward for word of Moking's whereabouts. Someone must know where he has gone, and I pray that his greed will outweigh his fear of him.'

But his prayer went unanswered, and Ashley grew increasingly anxious. More than Caro's safety was troubling him. Unpleasant rumours were circulating in London about his marriage. According to the story making the rounds of the ton, Vinson, that prime catch, had inexplicably shackled himself to an antidote.

The ton had been assured that this was so by no less an authority than Sir Percival Plymtree, who had the advantage of actually having seen her. His cruel tongue had found a way to repay Caro for what he held to be her grievous insult to him, and he made the most of this opportunity.

He had been aided in this endeavour by Olive Kelsie. In her rage at having her plans thwarted, she had written Plymtree that she had heard from Ashley's own lips that he had married Caro only because she had agreed never to interfere with his affair with his true love, Lady Roxley.

'Dearest Caroline is so besotted with him that she would have agreed to anything to shackle him,' she had written. 'Silly child. He found her so boring that he fled from Bellhaven to London and his mistress within a fortnight of the nuptials, leaving the poor thing behind.'

With malicious delight, Sir Percival broadcast the contents of this letter far and wide, and all of London was soon talking about poor Lady Vinson.

Her husband tried to kill this cruel story by making a point of confiding to several of London's most notorious gossips that he had married so hastily because Levisham, who was on his deathbed, had wanted to see Caro wed before his demise. And, dutiful daughter that she was, she could not now leave her dying father to come to London.

But Vinson's explanation was soon made to seem ludicrous by a notice in the *Gazette*, which announced that his dying father-in-law had married Abigail Foster a week earlier. It was the first inkling Ashley had of the marriage, and he was furious. It confirmed to him that he had been tricked into marrying Caro and then into leaving her behind at Bellhaven. Strangely, he was far more upset by the latter than by the former. As the days since his return to London became weeks, he found that he missed his wife more than he could ever have suspected he would.

Within ten minutes of reading the *Gazette* announcement, Ashley had posted an angry letter to Levisham, announcing that he would be coming to Bellhaven to bring Caro to London in order to quiet the unfortunate rumours about her and their marriage. He wrote bluntly, trying to anticipate the arguments Levisham would raise against her leaving Bellhaven.

Do not try to fob my request off by saying that Caro is not yet ready to be presented to society. Although Caro lacks conduct, I have asked my mother to come to London to take her in hand and help to launch her. Mama and I will contrive to get her through this ordeal as painlessly as possible.

I permitted my wife to remain at Bellhaven because of your plea that you did not want to die alone. But, since you have now married, you are clearly no longer alone or dying. I know that Caro does not wish to come to London, but I have every confidence that you will find a way to convince her that she must, just as you found a way to hoax us into marrying.

Having vented his anger in his message to his father-in-law, Ashley wrote a second, calmer letter to his mother, asking her to come immediately to London.

When the Viscount's letter reached Bellhaven, Levisham read it with consternation. For the first time he confessed to Abigail the full story of how he had got Ashley to marry Caro.

'Now he realises you tricked him, and he is enraged,' Abigail said, frowning. 'I pray he will not take it out on Caro.'

'I pray not, too. How often I have wondered these past weeks whether I made a dreadful mistake in arranging this marriage,' the Marquess said grimly. He told his wife of Vinson's humiliating insistence that Caro swear to him she would never vex him about his mistress.

Abigail was appalled by the bargain her husband had struck with Vinson. The Viscount clearly cared only for his mistress. Furthermore, Abigail knew Vinson's taste in women, and Caro could not have been more different from the kind of woman he would have been expected to marry. Levisham had never seen Lady Roxley, but Abigail knew what an irresistible creature she was to men. No wife could ignore such a ravishing rival unless she had no feeling at all for her husband. But this was not the case with Caro. Her affections were more engaged than perhaps even she herself suspected.

Abigail knew at first hand the heartbreak of a woman who must live for years with the knowledge that the only man she would ever love was obsessed with another woman. The only way to survive with dignity was to pretend, as Abigail herself had done, that one did not care. She thought of poor Lady Yarwood, hanging so desperately, so pathetically, on to a husband who did not want her. Caro had to be warned against doing that.

'She will not want to go to London,' the Marquess fretted. 'If I tell her that Vinson insists on it, she will tease him to let her remain here, and that will further anger him. I shall have to tell her that it is I who insists she go.'

Summoning Caro, Levisham told her, 'I have ordered your husband to Bellhaven.'

'What?' she gasped, her heart leaping at the thought of seeing Ashley again. 'Why?'

'So that he may take you back to London with him.'

Caro's happiness dissolved. She doubted that Ashley would even come, but if he did, what would his reaction be to having his unwanted wife foisted on him so soon? No doubt he had expected her to remain at Bellhaven for many weeks.

'I do not want to go to London!' she protested vehemently. 'I want to stay here at Bellhaven with you.'

'It is your duty to be at your husband's side. He was kind enough to let you remain with me when I was so ill, but I am much improved. We can no longer use my illness as an excuse to keep you here. Furthermore, I now have a wife to care for me.'

Caro, struggling to hold back the tears that threatened, was wounded to the core that her father was so anxious to be rid of her now that he had re-married. That was why he was sending her to a husband who did not want her, either. Never before in her life had she felt so useless, lonely and unwanted.

Her sensibilities suffered another wound when her father proceeded to lecture her on how she was to behave in London so that she would not give her husband a disgust of her.

'I fear I have been too easy on you, Caro, excusing your unladylike behaviour, but now you must act like a young matron of the first respectability. You cannot embarrass your husband.'

'I—I would never deliberately embarrass Ashley, Papa,' she stammered, 'but I do not know how a matron of the first respectability acts.'

'First, you must learn to mind your tongue, pet. As for the rest, Vinson has asked his mama to take you in hand and teach you. See that you obey her in everything she says.'

Caro's heart sank. Knowing what a stiff high stickler his father was, she could only assume that his mama was cut from the same cloth and would be even more rigid in her expectations than Aunt Olive had been. A frightening thought struck her: would life with Ashley's mother be any great improvement over that with Aunt Olive?

Later, when Abigail asked Caro if she was happy that she would soon be seeing her husband, she replied dejectedly, 'If he comes.'

'But of course he will come! You are his wife, and he wants you at his side.'

'I am not the wife he wants,' Caro said unhappily.

Fearing that Caro was right, Abigail did not dispute this. She would not raise false hopes in her stepdaughter's heart. Instead, she gently explained that Caro must always treat her husband with the utmost amiability and politeness but must take great care not to hang on him tiresomely. There was nothing more pathetic than an unloved wife making a fool of herself over her indifferent husband.

'When you are in London, observe Lady Yarwood, and you will understand what I am talking about,' Abigail said. 'You must not expect your husband to dance attendance on you, and above all, never take notice of his other connection.'

Tears welled up in Caro's eyes. 'I am so miserable when I think of Ashley with Lady Roxley.'

Abigail hugged her comfortingly. 'Of course you are! But you must remember your promise to him and not plague him about her.'

Caro nodded unhappily. She sincerely doubted that Ashley would even heed her father's summons to come for his unwanted wife.

Three days later, Caro was reading quietly in the library when she heard the butler greet Ashley. The sound of his voice sent tremors of excitement and happiness through her. He had come! He had come! She tossed her book aside and ran into the hall, where he stood in his brown travelling-coat, his curly black hair ruffled by the wind, smiling that irresistible smile of his. It was hard for Caro to believe that such a magnificent creature was her husband. Her eyes sparkled with pleasure at the sight of him.

Suddenly he held out his arms to her. In her excitement at seeing him, she rushed into them and they closed round her, making her feel as though she were in heaven. His lips descended on hers in a long, tender kiss that took her breath away. Even after he lifted his mouth from hers, she continued to hug him so fiercely that finally he said drily, 'I do believe, elfin, that you are happy to see me.'

She pulled away from him, looking up at his smiling face, her cheeks reddening in embarrassment at her foolish display. 'I cannot imagine that the same is true of you,' she observed candidly, a hint of bitterness in her tone.

Looking startled, he hugged her to him again, retorting gallantly, 'I did not think you had such a paltry imagination, elfin. Of course I am happy to see you.'

She smiled shyly at his words, revelling in the feel of his arms about her.

'And delighted, too, to learn the good news about your father's marriage and vastly improved health.' Ashley's voice suddenly took on an inexplicably frosty tone, and there was a glint of anger in his eyes. 'That is why I have come to claim my bride.'

Caro's heart seemed to tumble to her little kid-shod feet. Ashley was angry because he had been summoned to take her to London. Feeling utterly unwanted, she protested, 'I do not wish to go. Nor can you want me to.'

'Who gave you that nonsensical idea?' he asked curtly.

All of Aunt Olive's criticisms came back to haunt Caro. Her eyes were grey pools of misery. 'I will embarrass you.'

'Nonsense! I shall be very proud of you,' he declared as though he meant it, but Caro knew that he could not. 'We will leave in the morning.'

She was devastated at the thought of leaving her home with a man who, although he was her husband, did not want her. 'Surely not so soon! I cannot possibly be ready. I must pack, and . . .'

'You need bring only an extra gown or two with you. Your present wardrobe is better suited to a schoolgirl than to a fashionable young London matron. I have taken the liberty of ordering a new one for you from Madame Balan.'

Seeing the startled, half-angry look in her eyes, he added with a disarming smile, 'I know it was presumptuous of me, elfin. But I promise you that you will like my taste better than your aunt's. And do not worry about a maid. My mother is engaging one for you in London.'

Caro was stung that he considered her such a child that she could not be trusted to engage her own maid. 'I do not wish to go to a city where I know no one,' she pleaded. 'I shall be so lonely.'

'No, you won't,' Ashley predicted. 'You will soon be caught up in such a social whirl that you will long for a respite from it. And I am persuaded that Mama and you will deal famously, elfin.'

Remembering Bourn's reaction to her, Caro knew that her husband was wrong. His mother would be as bad as Aunt Olive.

CHAPTER TWENTY-ONE

CARO came slowly awake, drowsily conscious of a jarring cacophony about her, a rough jolting beneath her, and strong, protective arms round her. Her eyes fluttered open, revealing the darkened burgundy velvet interior of Ashley's travelling coach. She stifled a groan. How long it took to reach London! She must have fallen asleep sitting upright on the cushions.

Now she was lying on her side against her husband, braced in the corner of the coach so that her head and upper body rested on his shoulder and muscular chest. The day, which had seemed promising when they had set out so early that morning, had quickly turned grey and blustery, and she saw that Ashley had tucked a travelling-rug round her to ward off any chill.

Cosseted like this in her husband's arms, Caro felt so comfortable, cherished and, above all, happy that she could not bring herself to move or even to confess that she was awake for fear that he might relinquish his protective hold. If only she could stay like this for ever!

Despite her languor, Caro could no longer ignore the clamour that attacked her ears. The heavy curtains of burgundy velvet had been pulled across the windows, creating an artificial twilight in the coach and preventing her from looking out. Above the din of horses' hooves pounding and carriage-wheels clanking on paved stones, a dissonant chorus of raucous voices was shouting, but Caro could make out only a word or two.

Puzzled, she lifted her head and discovered that Ashley was watching her. A smiling tenderness in his eyes made her heart beat in double time. Shyly, she returned his smile, and his lips settled over hers in a kiss so achingly sweet that her besieged heart seemed to stop beating altogether.

When you lose your heart to a man, you will like his kisses very much... You will yearn for them.

After their lips parted, she looked at him with eyes so wide that he laughed. 'Yes, elfin?' he asked, his green ones sparkling with amusement and something else that she could not define.

Her face reddened and she looked hastily away, too embarrassed to try to explain to him the exciting sensations that had buffeted her during their kiss.

Once again the din beyond the coach intruded on her consciousness. 'What—What is all that noise?' she asked shakily.

'That, my elfin, is London.' Ashley reached up to open one of the curtains that he had drawn when she fell asleep.

Sitting up, Caro pressed her face eagerly to the glass for her first glimpse of the metropolis. Her initial impression was of a profusion of conveyances—carriages, curricles, carts, horses—and of people, most of whom seemed to be shabbily dressed and shouting at the top of their voices.

Ashley's coach, caught in this confusion, had slowed to a crawl.

'Why are they yelling so?' she asked.

'They are pedlars, hawking their wares. See the woman with her overskirt pinned up... she is selling

spoons. The man next to her is an oystermonger. The
woman holding her hat in front of her has it filled
with cherries. Listen carefully, and you will be able
to make out some of the different items.'

She did as Ashley instructed. Slowly, her ears
became more accustomed to the strange sounds, and
she was able to pick out cries of watercress, rabbits
and gingerbread for sale.

'Is London always so noisy?' she asked apprehensively. 'I shall never sleep again.'

'Our home is in a quieter neighbourhood.'

Our home. The words thrilled her. So did the
comfort of her husband's arms about her. She never
wanted to relinquish them—not to Lady Roxley, not
to any woman!

The carriage turned a corner, and Caro's nose
wrinkled in distaste as it was suddenly assailed by
strong, stomach-wrenching smells.

Noticing her expression, Ashley signalled to his
coachman to stop at a flower girl's stall. Its profusion
of violets, roses and yellow and orange wallflowers
provided a brilliant splash of colour to the drab street.
Ashley chose a bouquet of pink moss roses and green
mignonette. As the carriage started up again, he presented it to Caro. 'Put it to your face,' he advised her.
'It will make the odour more bearable.'

Burying her nose in the flowers, Caro could no
longer discern anything but their sweet fragrance. She
was touched that he should have noticed her
discomfort.

*He will treat you always with the utmost kindness
and consideration if you do not plague him about his
other interest.*

Caro had removed her bonnet before she had fallen asleep. The coil in which she had fastened her uncontrollable hair had loosened during her nap, and now wayward strands drifted about her face as she sniffed her bouquet. Gently Ashley smoothed them back from her face, his touch sending a frisson through her.

'Your hair has a will of its own,' he observed.

'Yes,' she said ruefully, raising her head from her bouquet. 'If I had my way, I would have it all cut off.'

'I want you to have your way. I think your hair would look charming cut short and curled about your face,' he said, caressing her cheek lightly with his fingertip.

He is fond of you... If you strive to be the kind of wife Vinson wants, my pet, he might in time come to love you.

Caro's mouth tightened in determination. She would make Ashley a wife that he would be proud of, a wife that he would learn to love. But what kind of wife was that?

Ashley, noticing the questioning look in her eyes, said lazily, 'Yes, elfin?'

'What do you want of me?'

His emerald eyes blinked at her in surprise. 'What?'

'Oh, Ashley, I so want to be the kind of wife you wish for, but I don't known what that is.' Her eyebrows knit together in a woebegone frown. 'I suppose I must learn to become a lady of the first respectability.'

'Yes, I would like that, elfin,' he said, the gravity of his voice belied by the smile in his eyes. He tilted her chin up. 'I would also like another kiss,' he added, lowering his lips to hers. His fingertips, as light as a butterfly's wing, stroked her face, and this time Caro's arms crept round his neck and clung to him. His kiss grew more ardent, stirring exquisitely unsettling sensations in her.

When he lifted his mouth, he gazed into her eyes, still dreamy from the effect he had on her. 'I am persuaded, elfin, that you no longer find kissing repulsive.'

'Not with you,' she murmured, her voice as languid as her gaze.

He frowned. 'Was there someone with whom it was repulsive?'

She looked away, remembering that she had given Tilford her word.

'Caro, answer me,' her husband insisted. 'Was it Tilford?'

'How did you know?'

He ignored her question. 'Tell me what happened.'

She did, including the promise not to tell that her cousin had extracted from her. When she finished, her husband looked so furious that she asked uneasily, 'Why are you so angry at me?'

'Not you, elfin. Your cousin. I promise you that it will not be like that with me.' Ashley folded her into his arms and held her tightly, as though he meant to protect her from the world. She nestled happily against him.

It was some moments before Ashley spoke again. 'I thought that tonight we would dine quietly at home with my mother. It will give you an opportunity to become acquainted with her.'

Caro's happiness evaporated at the prospect of meeting the Countess. It was hard for Caro to decide which she dreaded more: meeting her ladyship or being introduced to London society.

But a half-hour in her mother-in-law's company was more than enough to prove to Caro that her grim expectations had been an unforgivable slander of the Countess. She was quite the most vivacious and charming woman that Caro had ever met, and so youthful-looking that when her daughter-in-law first saw her, she thought that Ashley had neglected to mention that he had a sister. It was from his mother that Ashley had inherited his curly dark hair and laughing emerald eyes, his charm and his amiability.

Instead of looking askance at her plain, awkward little daughter-in-law, the Countess greeted her with the warmest of hugs. 'You poor darling, you must be fagged to death after such a trip! And apprehensive, too, about what awaits you in a strange city where you know no one. But do not fret yourself about it. My son and I will take very good care of you.'

Having grown up motherless, with Aunt Olive as her only maternal example, Caro was quite unprepared for Lady Bourn's understanding and solicitude.

Ashley installed his wife in a charming apartment furnished with exquisitely delicate pieces of French furniture that seemed scaled to her own tiny size. The walls were draped with a lovely peach silk moiré that was also used for the bed hangings. It was quite the loveliest set of rooms she had ever seen. When she told Ashley and his mother this, he looked very pleased.

'My son chose both the hangings and the furniture himself,' the Countess confided. 'The workmen have been here from dawn to late in the night to finish it before your arrival.'

'Surely you did not have it redecorated just for me?' Caro asked in disbelief.

'Most certainly he did,' the Countess answered for him. 'And I have engaged an excellent French maid for you. Unfortunately she cannot start until the day after tomorrow. However, she comes with the most glowing recommendations. I am persuaded that she is precisely what you wanted, Ashley.''

Caro wondered uneasily what precisely it was that her husband had wanted in her maid: a quasi-guardian, perhaps, to keep a close watch over her so that she did not embarrass him.

Her spirits immediately rose, however, as she looked at the bowl of daisies on the small secretaire, the chrysanthemums on the French commode, and the vases of white roses by her bedside and on the mantel of the fireplace. Ashley had kept his promise to her that she would not lack for flowers in London.

'The ton is agog with curiosity over Caro,' the Countess said. 'We will be inundated with invitations when it is learned she is in town.'

As if reading her thoughts, Ashley took Caro's hand in his and squeezed it comfortingly. 'Do not fret, elfin. We shall neither go into society nor accept callers immediately. My intention is to introduce you at Lady Jersey's ball a fortnight from now. By then you shall be ready to bear the ton.'

'I shall never be ready!' Caro exclaimed with strong conviction.

He smiled. 'I promise you will.'

Dinner that night was a pleasant affair. Ashley and his mama took pains to draw Caro into their lively exchanges, and by the time the covers were removed, all her shyness towards her mother-in-law had vanished.

When it came time to retire, Ashley took her arm and led her upstairs. 'How do you like Mama, elfin?'

'She is marvellous! I cannot imagine her being married to your pa—' Caro broke off, realising the quagmire into which her candid tongue was leading her.

Instead of taking umbrage, Ashley laughed. 'I think marrying my mother was the only unexpected thing my father ever did. But, strangely, for two such opposites, they are very happy together. He dotes on her.'

When they reached her apartment, Caro was trying to hide a large yawn behind her hand.

'Poor elfin. Are you exhausted?'

'Yes,' she admitted. 'I cannot wait to tumble into bed and fall asleep.'

Opening the door to her apartment, he said, 'Then I shall bid you good night, unless there is something that you might like me to do for you.'

Caro regarded him with innocent, uncomprehending eyes. 'Nothing,' she assured him, covering another yawn with her hand.

Puzzled by the disappointment that clouded his face, she hastened to reassure him. 'You have done so much already. It is the most beautiful bedroom I have ever seen.' She tried to stifle another yawn, but was unsuccessful.

'Get into bed, elfin, before you fall asleep standing up. You have a busy day ahead of you tomorrow. Your first fittings at Madame Balan's are scheduled. Good night, and sweet dreams,' Ashley said, bending to give her a kiss that did much to ensure such dreams. 'I will see you in the morning.'

CHAPTER TWENTY-TWO

LADY ROXLEY had heard nothing from Ashley since her children had arrived in London, and with each passing day she grew increasingly concerned and incredulous. Why did he not come? Nothing was going the way Estelle had anticipated.

Then Sir Percival Plymtree's version of Vinson's marriage reached her interested ears, and she asked him to call on her so that she might hear it from his own lips.

'You need not worry, beautiful Estelle,' he assured her. 'No man, especially not a man of Vinson's taste, is going to lose his heart to that farouche creature. She so bored him that he left her behind and fled back to London.'

Estelle was delighted. 'How humiliating for her!'

'To give Vinson credit, he did concoct some Banbury tale about her remaining behind at Bellhaven because her father was dying.' Sir Percival gave a loud sniff. 'What a faradiddle that was! As I have been quick to point out to everyone, Levisham made such an immediate and remarkable recovery that he married again a fortnight after Vinson's departure from Bellhaven. That hardly sounds like a man at death's door.'

'The Marquess cannot be happy about Ashley deserting his daughter before the ink is dry on their marriage certificate,' Estelle observed.

'Of course he is not. I wager that is why Vinson brought her to London yesterday.'

'She's here?' Estelle exclaimed, consumed by curiosity to see her lover's wife.

'But don't expect to see them soon. They are not receiving callers or accepting any invitations at present.' Plymtree gave a nasty little laugh. 'Vinson is clearly too embarrassed to introduce his poor awkward wife to society. I hear that he has ordered her a lavish wardrobe from Madame Balan, to be completed in such great haste that the first fittings are scheduled for this afternoon. But it will take more than even Balan's genius to make that antidote presentable.'

Estelle, eager to reassure herself with her own eyes of Caro's unattractiveness, smiled at this bit of intelligence. Perhaps she, too, would pay Madame Balan a visit that afternoon.

Caro, watching Lady Bourn descend from her carriage and glide as lightly as a cloud towards the door of Madame Balan's shop in Charlotte Street, was determined to copy the Countess's graceful walk.

In the short time that she had known her mother-in-law, Caro had come to regard this charming, bubbly woman with love and awe. The Countess even professed to be amused, rather than shocked, by her daughter-in-law's candid tongue, and encouraged her confidences with understanding and sympathy.

Caro followed her mother-in-law into the elegant shop. Exquisite examples of Madame's wares—ball-gowns, morning dresses, riding-habits, even a wedding dress—were on display in the showroom. Next to them, Caro felt exceedingly dowdy and out of place in her plain, skimpy gown of blue cambric.

A pretty young woman in a spotted muslin gown
that was surely another one of Madame's creations
presided over the showroom. It had been outfitted like
a large, opulent sitting-room with Louis Quinze chairs
and sofas. A round rosewood table covered with
sketches of Madame's designs caught Caro's eye.

The young woman, recognising the Countess, said
that Madame Balan wished Milady to try on her new
ball-gown before beginning the extensive fitting her
daughter-in-law's new wardrobe would require.

Lady Bourn, seeing Caro's interest in the sketches,
suggested that she remain behind to examine them for
styles that she liked. Caro took a chair at the rosewood
table while her mother-in-law disappeared through a
curtained door. Caro knew from Grace and Jane that
all of London's best-dressed ladies patronised
Madame Balan's.

The young woman in the spotted muslin asked
whether Caro would like tea. When she replied in the
affirmative, the girl also disappeared through the curtained doorway.

After studying the sketches for some minutes, Caro
rose from the table to examine more closely the in-
tricately jewelled bodice of a satin ball-gown displayed nearby. Hearing the door to the shop open
behind her, she turned to behold the most ravishingly
beautiful woman she had ever seen. Her face, with
its lustrous complexion, seemed perfect in every
feature, as did her form, which was elegantly displayed in a perfectly fitted gown of amethyst silk that
was the same shade as her fascinating eyes.

Caro could only stare at this dazzling woman, who
returned her scrutiny with equal interest, making Caro
acutely conscious of how ugly and awkward she

looked by comparison. This intense mutual inspection continued for a long moment before the
stranger's amethyst eyes glowed with an unholy delight that startled Caro. The stranger turned abruptly
and left the shop without a word.

Through the window, Caro saw her enter a handsomely lacquered carriage that had drawn up in front
of Ashley's.

Caro was still puzzling over the beauty's odd behaviour when she was led to a fitting-room, where she
quickly forgot the woman and all else but the
wardrobe that her husband had chosen for her.

Unlike the gowns that her aunt had selected, these
were artfully designed to capitalise on her tiny figure,
making her look daintily petite instead of awkwardly
boyish. It was an exciting revelation to Caro to see
how much more attractive she looked in them. And
the colours became her, too. There were no pinks or
bright yellows or purples or blacks, the shades her
aunt had always selected because they became her
daughters so well. Instead, Ashley had chosen salmon,
deep peach, gold and other shades that brought out
the warmth of Caro's skin tones rather than making
her look sallow.

Perhaps there was hope for her yet, she thought,
more determined than ever to become a wife Ashley
would be proud of.

When Caro and her mother-in-law returned home,
a hairdresser was waiting. After a consultation with
Ashley, he cut her hair. When he was finished, her
very short locks, looking darker and richer now that
the faded ends had been cut away, curled charmingly
about her face, softening it so that she now looked
like a mischievous pixie.

As she stared in amazement at her new reflection in the mirror, she exclaimed to Ashley, 'How different I look! And it is such a relief to be rid of all that dreadful hair.'

That night when Ashley led Caro upstairs, he followed her into her apartment.

She turned to him happily. 'Thank you again for my beautiful gowns. I love them all.'

He smiled, clearly pleased. 'You are entirely welcome. Madame Balan has promised to deliver a completed riding-habit tomorrow afternoon. Would you like to go riding in the park with me the following morning?'

'Oh, yes!' Caro cried, clapping her hands in delight. She had loved her morning rides with Ashley at Bellhaven. 'Can we ride every morning?'

'I think, elfin, after you go into society, you will prefer to sleep later in the morning and ride in the afternoon with the rest of the ton.'

'But I like it when there is no one about but us.'

He smiled. 'So do I, elfin. Since your maid does not arrive until tomorrow, I had better help you with the buttons on your dress. I do not believe you can manage them by yourself.'

Ashley was right. She was wearing a high-necked muslin gown fastened by a long row of tiny cloth buttons that extended down her back.

Ashley's hands gently touched the back of her neck. A tiny shudder of excitement shook Caro. When he had opened the first few buttons, his lips caressed the nape of her neck, so exquisitely sensitive to his touch, with soft kisses. Then, after skilfully undoing the lower fastenings, his lips followed his fingers down her back, tracing it with more kisses. His mouth returnèd to nuzzle her neck and ear as his hands slipped between the gown and her shift. He gently stroked her belly, sending shock waves through her. A moan of pleasure, which seemed to have been wrenched from the depths of her soul, escaped from her lips.

'Shall I bid you good night, elfin?' he whispered, his seductive voice very close to her ear, tickling it with his warm breath.

'What are you doing to me?' She gasped as his hands, moving with tantalising slowness, cupped her small, firm breasts, sending a tongue of fire licking through her.

'Giving you a hint of the pleasure a husband can bring to his wife.' He turned her round so that she faced him, and his lips claimed hers in a kiss that was deeper, more demanding, and more thrilling than any he had yet given her.

When he lifted his mouth, she could only stare up at him in mute wonder at what he had stirred within her. His gleaming green eyes stared down into hers. 'What is it you want, elfin?'

She stared at him, mesmerised by his eyes and his touch. He took a step away from her, and she swayed towards him, a silent entreaty in her eyes.

He smiled. 'Shall I stay with you tonight, elfin?'

She nodded, helpless before her yearning for him.

Caro stirred and came drowsily awake as she felt the arm that held her in an embrace that was both possessive and protective. Memories of the night with Ashley, so sweet and satisfying, swept through her, filling her with warmth and consuming happiness.

Her eyes fluttered open. Light had crept into the room around the edges of the heavy curtains. Beside her, Ashley stirred and tightened his hold on her, his body exuding an inviting warmth in the coolness of dawn. Caro stared lovingly at his features, barely discernible in the faint illumination. In repose, he looked like a young boy, his face relaxed and his thick dark hair tousled.

Caro closed her eyes and smiled dreamily. The night had been worth waiting for. So different from what she could ever have dreamed of after her experience with Tilford.

Ashley had told her that it would be different with him and, as usual, he had been right. He had been so tender and gentle with her, slowly caressing and teasing her until she thought she would die from the turbulent desires that he stoked in her. Only then had he allowed her a satisfaction that exploded in an incandescent burst, that had left her stunned and blissfully content.

But why had he, having married her only for an heir, waited so long to make her fully his? Was she so unattractive to him? This question revived all her insecurities about her marriage.

Gentle fingertips lightly brushed her cheek. 'What are you thinking about, elfin?' Ashley's voice was deep and groggy.

She had thought him asleep, and her eyes flew open in surprise at the sound of his voice. 'Last night,' she admitted.

Concern creased his face. 'Then why the frown? Did you not like it?'

She made no attempt to hide her feelings. 'It was so wonderful that I wondered why you waited so long.'

'I was afraid that I would frighten you, elfin,' he answered simply. 'I wanted to be certain that you were comfortable with me and wished for my attention first.'

Her eyes widened in surprise at his unexpected answer. 'Truly?'

'Truly, elfin,' he replied, kissing her tenderly.

Caro's heart swelled with love for him, and she silently renewed her vow to be the kind of wife he wanted.

CHAPTER TWENTY-THREE

ON THE night of Lady Jersey's ball, Caro glided down the wide curving staircase of Bourn House to the entrance hall, where she caught sight of herself in one of the big gilt-framed mirrors. She could scarcely believe that the image of the singularly striking young lady reflected there could possibly be herself. How different she looked from the girl who had arrived at Bourn House only a fortnight ago!

This change, which Caro viewed as nothing short of miraculous, she owed to her new French maid, Hélène, her mother-in-law and, most of all, her husband.

Hélène had very lightly applied her magic from various mysterious jars and bottles to highlight Caro's eyes, fine high cheekbones and pretty mouth.

To Lady Bourn, Caro owed a new-found grace of movement and confidence of manner.

It was Ashley who had selected the peach satin gown, the most flattering she had ever owned in her life, that she wore tonight. And it was Ashley who had given her the special glow of a woman deeply in love who has been well loved in return.

The door to the library opened, and he came into the hall. His blue evening coat, cut away at the waist, and black pantaloons had been tailored to fit his long, trim body with its slim hips and muscular shoulders. A white silk waistcoat, embroidered with silver, peeked from beneath the coat.

Seeing her, his eyes glowed with obvious appreciation. 'How lovely you look tonight, elfin,' he said.

'You and Hélène have performed a miracle. You have made me pretty.'

'No,' he demurred. 'You were always pretty, elfin. We have shown you how to reveal it. Your aunt worked so hard to conceal it.'

As Caro rode with Ashley and her mother-in-law to Lady Jersey's ball for her début into society, she faced the night ahead with an assurance that she had not possessed a fortnight ago. Still, she could not help being nervous at the thought of being introduced to the denizens of the Polite World. Lady Bourn had said that the ball would be an enormous squeeze. Everyone would be there. Caro so wanted them, and, above all, Ashley himself, to think her a wife worthy of him.

You must learn to mind your tongue.

Turning worried eyes to her husband, Caro promised in a subdued voice, 'I will try very hard to curb my tongue tonight so that I do not embarrass you.'

'No, I pray that you do not do so on my account, elfin. It is part of your charm, and you will not embarrass me. As a modish young matron, you will have more licence to speak your mind than when you were an unmarried girl. Do not censor yourself, and most particularly not on my account.'

'Truly?'

'Truly!' He grinned at her. 'I promised you that I would be a an easy husband.'

Yes, he was, and a most satisfying one, too. He had spent a great deal of time with her since their arrival in London, acting to perfection the role of attentive, doting husband. She had treasured those hours with him. Each day she had grown more in love with him.

Now, as their carriage stopped in front of Lady Jersey's, Caro thought that she had never been happier in her life.

When they were announced, Caro suddenly felt as though every eye was upon her. And she was right. The unflattering stories that Sir Percival had circulated about her and her marriage, coupled with her delayed introduction to society, had made her the chief topic of conversation among the ton. An appearance by Princess Charlotte, the Regent's daughter and heir, could not have created more of a stir.

Ashley's reassuring arm about her and his warm smile of encouragement quickly shored up Caro's confidence, and she gracefully made her way into the ballroom, her head held high. She would permit no one to guess how nervous she was.

The newly-weds were soon surrounded by those eager to judge for themselves the much-talked-about bride. Caro was introduced to so many people in rapid succession that her mind whirled and her head ached. To her relief, Ashley, at his most charming, guided the conversation into light, amusing channels. After a time, she began to relax and actually, to her amazement, to enjoy herself.

Ashley never left her side, hovering beside her with a tender solicitude towards her that confounded the gossips, who were watching the newly-weds with eagle eyes. There was nothing in Ashley's manner towards his wife that bespoke an unwanted marriage with a woman who bored him.

Caro, too, was a surprise. She was not a beauty in the conventional sense, but she was very striking with those large, expressive eyes and delicate gamine face. Although she had an amusingly candid tongue, the want of conduct that Sir Percival had accused her of was nowhere in evidence. His tales about her and her hasty marriage were soon discounted as another example of his malicious tongue. After all, the way Vinson hovered about her, anyone could see that he cared deeply for his bride.

Which was what Ashley, determined to put to rest the rumours circulating about his wife and his marriage, intended.

Several times during the course of the evening, Caro noticed another young woman, quite plain, with a shy air about her, whom Caro judged to be three or four years older than herself. When Caro first saw the girl, she was on the arm of a dashing young man whom she clearly adored, for she never removed her eyes from him. Even while they were conversing with other couples, her eyes continued to watch only him even when their companions were talking.

When her escort attempted to break away from her, she clutched desperately at his sleeve. Although Caro was too far away to hear what passed between them, the man was clearly furious at her. Finally, she released her hold on his sleeve, and he stalked away. Her eyes, filled with tears, continued to watch him wherever he moved. Whenever Caro saw her after that, her gaze was still fixed on the young man who had not once returned to her side.

Late in the evening, the girl went timidly up to the young man and plucked at his sleeve. He rounded on her angrily, clearly berating her. Seeing the misery in her eyes, Caro's heart went out to her.

'Who is that girl?' Caro asked her mother-in-law, who was talking to the Duchess of Stratford. Ashley had gone off to find them refreshments.

'That's Lady Yarwood, poor thing,' the Countess replied. 'Her husband married her only for her fortune, but she, unfortunately, worships him.'

So that was poor Lady Yarwood, Caro thought, remembering what Abigail had said about her.

'If only she would not hang on her husband so,' the Duchess said. 'It is not at all the thing to do. She succeeds only in giving him a greater disgust of her. It is quite pathetic.'

Abigail had said nearly the same thing. Remembering her stepmother's warning, Caro resolved never to hang on Ashley.

Although it was late, well past the time when guests were still being announced, a new arrival swept in the door. It was the breathtakingly beautiful woman that Caro had seen at Madame Balan's. She wore a ruby satin gown that emphasised her exotic beauty, and she drew openly appreciative glances from the men about the entrance. Curious, Caro asked her mother-in-law and the Duchess who the woman was.

Seeing her, the Duchess drew in her breath sharply, and the charming Countess seemed at a loss for words. Finally, she said blandly, 'That is Lady Roxley, Sir Fletcher's wife.' Lady Bourn was clearly unaware that Caro knew the identity of her husband's mistress.

The Duchess hastily changed the subject, and neither woman noticed the shattering effect this revelation had on Caro. The world seemed to dissolve into a blur around her. She could not see and she felt as though she could not breathe, either. So this was her rival for Ashley's love! All that she had heard

about Lady Roxley's beauty had not done it justice.
Her rival, Caro thought bitterly. What a joke that was.
There was no way a plain, skinny thing like herself
could compete with that sublime creature. The hard-
won self-assurance that Caro had gained in recent days
dissolved in an instant. A lump the size of a grape-
fruit rose in her throat, and she wanted nothing so
much as to flee from the ballroom.

She saw the beautiful amethyst eyes scanning the
room, looking for someone. Then Lady Roxley's gaze
alighted on Ashley, who was directing a servant carrying a tray of champagne glasses towards his mother
and his wife. She hurried up to him with a brilliant
smile. Taking his hand, she pulled him towards a door
that led to a small withdrawing-room.

Caro slipped away from her mother-in-law, who was
so engrossed in her conversation with the Duchess that
she did not notice. Scarcely aware of what she was
doing, Caro made her way towards the door through
which her husband and his mistress had disappeared.
As Caro reached it, she saw Ashley, his back to her,
talking to Lady Roxley.

Triumph was plain in that lady's face and in the
timbre of her low, sultry voice. 'Poor Ashley, all of
London is buzzing about what a plain little waif your
wife is.' She fluttered her fan seductively. 'But I
confess, my love, that I am glad that she is, for now
I need never worry about her stealing your love from
me.'

'No,' Ashley said in a strangled voice that Caro
hardly recognised, 'you need not fear that you *will*
lose my love to Caro...'

His wife could not bear to hear another word. Her
heart breaking, she turned and fled. *No, he does not*

want *to marry you any more than you do him...*
Vinson must marry—his father insists on it—and the
lady you mentioned is already wed to another. He
needs a wife to give him an heir...

All the happiness and joy that Caro had felt in
Ashley's arms during the past fortnight exploded in
a blinding white heat of disillusionment that left in
its wake only the bitter grey ash of burned-out hope
and dreams.

She hurried along the edge of the ballroom to the
hall and then into a small sitting-room, where she
threw herself down on a sofa, buried her head in her
hands, and sobbed in despair and grief. What a silly,
naïve fool she had been to think that she could win
her husband's love away from such a dazzling woman.

CHAPTER TWENTY-FOUR

IT WAS A long time before Caro managed to staunch her tears and an even longer time before she returned to the ballroom, an aching void in her heart.

What a fool's paradise she had lived in during the past fortnight. She had been told before she met Ashley that he made love charmingly. Now she could testify to the truth of that. It had lulled her into forgetting that a man did not have to love a woman to make love to her. Caro was, she realised bitterly, merely another one of his conquests. His heart still belonged to Lady Roxley.

Yet Caro could not ask for a gentler, more considerate husband. He had had to marry for an heir. But he had not had to marry *her*. He had been kind enough to do so to save her from Tilford, and now he was treating her with every courtesy, carefully concealing behind his ardent attentions that he did not love her.

Within a few days, his tender, skilled lovemaking had washed away all of Caro's apprehensions and inhibitions, and she had gone wild in his arms. Her face burned with shame as she remembered the stunned look on her husband's face the first time that it had happened. Terrified that such abandon was not at all the thing for a lady and had given Ashley a disgust of her, she had asked anxiously, 'Why do you look so—so strange?'

'I am amazed by what a passionate little thing you are,' he had replied gravely.

Little thing! 'I am not a child!'

'No, you are not, elfin,' he had said, an odd timbre to his voice, and had pulled her tightly against him. 'Go back to sleep.'

The comfort of his arms about her had quieted her doubts momentarily, and she had drifted off immediately.

But now, after overhearing him assure his mistress that she, not his wife, would always have his love, Caro was ashamed of her uninhibited behaviour in his arms that betrayed as surely as words her feelings for him, while all he wanted from her was a son.

Caro was determined never again to make a cake of herself over Ashley, in bed or out, causing him to be sorry that he had married her. She would not hang on him like a lovelorn schoolgirl, as Lady Yarwood did on her lord, pining for a love that he could not give her and sinking herself below reproach in his eyes.

Instead, Caro would follow her stepmother's advice and conduct herself as Abigail had with Levisham for so many years. Although she would be a model of amiability and politeness to her husband, she would treat him with a cool nonchalance that betrayed none of her feelings for him.

She would take care not to seem to want Ashley's love, or even to notice that she did not have it. It was not his fault that he could not love her—that his heart had been permanently engaged long before he had met her.

While this course of conduct would do nothing to ease the pain of her broken heart, at least her pride would not be in tatters. Her shoulders squared with

determination, Caro returned to the ballroom, vowing
to deceive the world—and her husband—into be-
lieving that she was having a magnificent time.

Deception did not come easily to her, but so determined was she that none of those many eyes
watching the spirited bride suspected that anything
might be amiss. Her performance, which would have
rivalled one of Mrs Siddons's at her zenith, fooled
even her mother-in-law and her husband.

Caro entered into the London social whirl with a
gaiety and an enthusiasm that startled her husband.
He failed to detect the desperation in her determination to fill her time with an endless round of social
obligations. She was such a success that after a few
days her mother-in-law, seeing her triumphantly
launched in society, departed to rejoin her husband
at his country seat.

Caro quickly acquired a retinue of admirers who
surrounded her wherever she went. It was not long
before the more elderly of the ton were whispering
how much like her vibrant mama the young Lady
Vinson was. True, she was not the great beauty the
late Marchioness had been, but was quite pretty in
her own way, and so like her mama in spirit, charm,
and outrageous tongue.

Although Ashley had expected his wife to be a hit,
he had not expected her to become a toast, yet that
was what was happening. Caro's popularity, coupled
with Ashley's doting attention to her in public, quickly
put to rest the stories circulating about why he had
married her.

Soon the gossips had a new and far more scandalous tale to occupy them. Lord Lewis, returning

unexpectedly to the city late one night from his country seat, found his wife absent from his London house and set out to find her. His quest ended in the bedchamber of his young son's handsome dancing-master, Mr Nickerson, whose greatest talents reputedly were not on the dance-floor. A duel was fought on the spot, ending in the demise of Mr Nickerson. Outraged not so much by his wife's infidelity as by her inelegant choice of lovers, his lordship threatened divorce.

Attempting to retain her reputation and her husband, his lady insisted that she had no notion of how she had come to wake up in the late Mr Nickerson's bed. The last thing she recalled was chancing to meet him, carrying two glasses of wine, as she was strolling down one of the paths at Vauxhall. He offered her one of the glasses, saying he could not find the lady for whom he had fetched it. Accepting it, she drank a little wine and quickly became very dizzy.

She remembered nothing after that until she was awakened by her husband's arrival in Mr Nickerson's rooms. Clearly she had been drugged and abducted. Although the accused abductor was no longer alive to contradict her story, not a soul believed such a hum. It and its teller quickly became the butt of considerable ridicule. With this tale to occupy itself, the ton soon forgot the clearly untrue rumours about the Vinsons' marriage.

Meanwhile, Ashley was as tender and solicitous towards his bride in private as public. Indeed, had Caro not overheard him with his mistress, she would have believed herself to be cherished, if not loved, by him, so attentive and devoted was he.

But now that she knew his attention to her was motivated by courtesy rather than affection, Caro found it increasingly painful. Above all, she did not want to seem pathetic by wearing her heart on her sleeve or hanging on him. As her circle of admirers grew, she increasingly kept Ashley at a distance, making it clear to him that his gallant attention to her was no longer necessary now that she had her own devoted court.

If he preferred his mistress to her, she would show him that she preferred her admirers to him, even though, in truth, none of them could measure up to her husband in her eyes. If only he could experience a little of the jealousy she felt whenever she thought of him with Lady Roxley.

But if Ashley did, he gave no sign of it. Initially, he had been clearly puzzled by her treatment of him, asking her what was wrong. But, having sworn that she would never vex him about his mistress, she could not answer. Instead, she professed ignorance of what he could be talking about.

He, in turn, grew cooler towards her and more distant. Although he remained unfailingly courteous, he no longer stopped at her room at night but continued along to his own. Which was just as well, for it had been during those most intimate moments that Caro found it most difficult to sustain her cool charade. Indeed, only the memory of what Ashley had told Lady Roxley kept her from failing miserably and betraying her true feelings.

He did not offer to squire her about as frequently as he had before. Caro, secretly yearning to have him at her side, soon found herself wishing her hapless escorts to Jericho. He was often gone at night, offering no explanation of where he had been. But Caro needed none. She knew that he was with Lady Roxley, and her nails would bite into the palms of her clenched hands.

Adding to Caro's misery was the realisation that Ashley did not seem to care in the slightest that she had attracted so many admirers. If only he would be jealous of her... But he was immune to that affliction where she was concerned. Or so Caro thought until the night at Lady Castleton's ball.

She arrived there on the arm of young Lord Aleem. Caro would rather have gone with Ashley, but not once during the past four days had he offered to escort her anywhere. She missed his company dreadfully, and found Aleem, who had just reached his majority, excessively boring compared to her husband.

Shortly after their arrival at Lady Castleton's, the hostess came up to her with a man who looked to be about forty. Despite a certain hardness to his features, Caro thought him very handsome for one of his advanced years. She had noticed him earlier in the evening when he had been surrounded by pretty women.

'This gentleman has been begging me to introduce you,' her ladyship said.

Caro's eyes widened in surprise. He was years older than her other admirers and had an air of cynicism about him that made her think he would prefer more sophisticated women than herself.

Seeing her reaction, he gave her a charming little bow. 'You see, I like to know my relatives, and your marriage has made you one.'

'Oh!' Caro exclaimed with dawning comprehension. 'You must be Henry Neel.'

The hard grey eyes narrowed. 'So your husband has told you about me. I suspect he was not flattering.'

'It was not he who told me of you.' When she had asked Lady Bourn about her husband's relatives, her mother-in-law had said that there was virtually none left except Henry, the family's black sheep, a distinction earned by his prodigious talents for gaming and seducing well-born ladies. Later, she had listened to the Countess and the Duchess of Carlyle discussing some of Henry's less admirable exploits.

Henry said mockingly, 'But, cousin, someone did tell you about me, and he was clearly not laudatory.'

Ever candid, Caro asked, 'Are you as bad as they say you are?'

'You must tell me how bad that is before I can answer,' he replied with a careless smile.

Intrigued by his indifference to his reputation, Caro observed, 'I do not believe you care in the slightest what anyone says about you.'

'You are as astute as you are pretty, *ma petite*.'

Rather flattered by this compliment, Caro allowed him to lead her to two red velvet *tabourets* along the wall, where he entertained her with subtle compliments intermixed with mocking comments on the personalities and peculiarities of their fellow guests. He was, she concluded, the most entertaining man, except for her husband, to be found in London. That was why she let him monopolise her for the remainder of the evening.

They were sitting in a quiet corner of the supper-room, enjoying cold chicken and champagne, when Ashley strode in. His face took on the dark aspect of a thundercloud when he saw his wife and his cousin.

He greeted Henry curtly, and told Caro, 'Come, we are leaving.'

'But...' she started to protest.

'I said, we are leaving,' he snapped in a tone that permitted no demur.

Once in their carriage, he was uncharacteristically silent on the ride home, sitting stiffly on the seat well apart from her. Casting him a surreptitious glance from beneath her lashes, she saw in the dim lamplight that his lips were drawn into a thin, angry line.

When they reached Bourn House, he escorted her to her room. Opening the door for her, he turned and momentarily blocked her way, informing her in the coldest tone she had yet heard from his lips that she was to have nothing more to do with Henry.

Caro's heart gave a little lurch of hope. 'Are you jealous of your cousin, my lord?' she asked.

'What a shatterbrained idea!' Ashley exclaimed disdainfully. 'Don't be ridiculous!'

His contemptuous response rankled Caro, who, despite it, was convinced that jealousy must be involved. 'Then why are you ordering me to stay away from him?'

'Because he is dangerous! His reputation with women is notorious. You are playing out of your league with him, child! Stick to the callow youths, such as young Aleem, who will do you no harm.'

Caro's anger boiled over at Ashley's calling her a child and at his dismissing her admirers as callow youths. 'I will associate with whom I please,' she cried, pushing furiously past him into her room.

Her defiance fired his own anger, and he snapped, 'Take care, Caro! I will not tolerate a wife who involves me or my name in a scandal!'

She whirled round, glaring at him. How dared he talk about her and scandal! What of him and Lady Roxley? Anger and jealousy overruled her good sense, and she cried, 'What will you do, my lord? Divorce me?'

'Yes!' he snapped. 'Remember that when next you flirt with my cousin!' He turned on his heel and was gone, slamming the door hard behind him.

CHAPTER TWENTY-FIVE

CARO, beset by tumultuous thoughts, lay awake until dawn lightened her room. Her thoughts oscillated between fear that Ashley might divorce her and rebellion at his treatment of her. How grossly unfair of him to demand of her a far more exacting standard of conduct than he embraced for himself!

Having no bosom bow or loving relative at hand to whom she could unburden her unhappiness over Ashley's liaison with Lady Roxley, she kept it locked up in her heart, where it had been festering. If only she could tell Ashley how miserable she was, but she had given her word that she would never vex him about Lady Roxley. Caro had made a bargain and now she must keep it.

At last she fell into a restless sleep. When she awakened late in the morning, Ashley had already left the house.

She asked Boothe when he was expected to return. 'Not until late, I dare say, for the Four-in-Hand Club meets today,' the butler replied.

'I dare say you are right,' Caro replied, trying to hide her disappointment. The club's members, including Lord Sefton with his bays, the Marquess of Worchester with his greys and Ashley with his chestnuts, assembled in Hanover Square for a spirited drive to the Windmill at Salt Hill, where they would partake of a magnificent dinner.

Ashley had not yet returned when Caro departed for a squeeze at Lady Farthe's. She left word where she had gone in the hope that her husband would follow her there.

Upon her arrival, Henry Neel immediately appeared at her side. Her thoughts, however, were so preoccupied with Ashley that she scarcely knew what Henry said to her. She kept looking towards the door in the hope that Ashley would appear, even though she knew how angry he would be if he saw her with his cousin. Her sorely wounded sensibilities still rebelled at his denying her a harmless flirtation with his cousin while he was committing far more scandalous acts with his mistress.

When at last, a few minutes before midnight, Ashley's tall figure appeared, Caro held her breath, caught between pleasure that he had come and anxiety over what he would do upon seeing her with his cousin.

What he did was turn on his heel and disappear into the card-room, leaving Caro blinking after him in disappointment. She did not seem him again that night. He was not yet home when she returned to Bourn House. He arrived a few moments after her, but his footsteps passed her door without pause on his way to his own.

During the next few days, she scarcely saw Ashley. He seemed always to be gone from home, and when they did chance to meet there, he greeted her curtly. To her horror, she realised that the breach between them was widening into a gulf.

She thought wistfully of all the good times they had had together before he had introduced her to society: their rides in the early morning; their billiard games;

their quiet times, full of laughter and good conversation, together. How she longed for those moments again.

Finally, desperate to have him to herself for a little while, she told him that she wished to resume riding in the park early in the morning as they had done when she first came to London. She expected Ashley to offer to accompany her. But, instead, he merely said coldly that he had no objection to her riding at that unconventional time so long as she was accompanied by a groom.

Disappointed, she none the less decided to avail herself of this opportunity, using the ride as an antidote to her intense unhappiness.

Although her husband neglected Caro, Henry did not. It occurred to Caro that since she had been introduced to him, he suddenly seemed to be everywhere that she was. More than coincidence had to be involved, and Caro, feeling flattered, rebelliously accepted his attentions. He was charming to her and most entertaining. Although he had about him the aura of danger and forbidden fruit, which makes a rakehell so irresistible to young, inexperienced girls, it was not that which attracted her. Rather, it was her conviction that her husband, even though he professed otherwise, was jealous of his cousin.

Caro did not, however, intend to be one of Henry's conquests and was careful never to be alone with him. When he learned of her morning rides in the park, he offered to accompany her, but she refused. When he began to press for more than her companionship at parties, she told him with her characteristic bluntness that she would never be unfaithful to her husband.

He left her abruptly, and she thought that would be the end of his attentions to her. But, to her surprise, he was back at her side the following night, acting the part of a perfect gentleman.

Caro would have been shocked to learn that she owed Henry's change of heart to Lady Roxley, on whom he had called earlier that day. It had been Henry's second visit to her ladyship.

His first call on Estelle had been on the day that Lady Castleton had introduced him to Caro.

On that day Lady Roxley had been seated at the three-legged bonheur du jour in her sitting-room, thinking how slowly time had passed for her since Lady Jersey's ball.

When Estelle had seen Caro at Madame Balan's, she had been overjoyed. The child was even worse than Percy Plymtree, who had never before been known to indulge in understatement, had said. No wonder Ashley was reluctant to introduce her to society. Estelle had left Madame Balan's secure in the conviction that Caro would never be her rival for Ashley's affection. Caro might have his name, but Estelle would always have his love.

So certain was she of this that the moment she had seen him at Lady Jersey's ball, she had insisted on leading him, despite his reluctance, to a little room where she could be private with him. There, she had put her arm about his neck and uttered those fatal words about never having to worry about Caro stealing his love away from her.

Her jubilation had vanished at the blazing anger in his eyes.

'No, you need not fear that you *will* lose my love to Caro,' he had said in a strangled voice, 'for you *have already done so.*'

He had jerked her arms from about his neck, his emerald eyes blazing like green fire. 'What an enormous debt of gratitude I owe my father for preventing me from marrying you!'

Before Estelle could recover from her shock, he had turned and stalked back into the ballroom.

At first, despite all the evidence to the contrary, she could not believe that she had actually lost him. But as the days turned into weeks and she heard nothing from him, she could no longer deny the truth. Her pride made her try to maintain the fiction that she and Ashley were still lovers. When gossips pointedly talked of how devoted he was to his bride, she intimated that despite his careful public front with Caro, he had discreetly increased his private attentions to his mistress. She was determined that she would do anything, no matter what, to get him back.

Then Henry Neel called to ask that she use her influence with Vinson to stop him from trying to connect Henry to William's death.

Estelle immediately remembered the nasty rumours that had circulated after William's fatal crash and the inquiry that had been held. Clearly, from what Henry said, Ashley now believed that his cousin had been involved. Although Estelle had never discussed this possibility with Ashley, she was careful to make Henry think otherwise. 'Will Ashley find the evidence he is seeking against you?'

'Unfortunately I have an associate who is an affidavit man. He will swear to whatever he thinks will be most rewarding to him. At the moment, he is enjoying a vacation in Wales at my expense, but Vinson is offering a large reward for information on his whereabouts. I fear it may be only a matter of time before someone sells it to him.'

That was when Estelle conceived her scheme to win Ashley back. At the very least, it would destroy his marriage and his wife's reputation. Ashley would never know of Estelle's involvement in his wife's ruin because Henry would be the instrument that carried it out.

Delighted with her own cleverness, Estelle immediately launched her plan with a pitying smile. 'You are a fool, Henry, if you think that I or anyone else could persuade Ashley to stop pursuing the truth about his brother's death. The best you can hope for is to force his silence or, failing that, discredit what he says about you in the eyes of the world.'

'And how the devil am I to do that? If I cannot stop him from asking questions, I can hardly force his silence on the answers. Even less could I discredit his word, for he is well known to be a man of integrity.'

'Let me tell you how.'

When Estelle finished, Henry said with reluctant admiration, 'What a diabolical woman you are! I cannot like using Vinson's wife as the instrument to obtain his silence.'

Estelle shrugged. 'It is the only instrument that you have. You know how the family abhors scandals involving their name.'

'True, but ...'

'I would not think that a man facing the gallows would have such scruples about using an instrument that can save him from them.'

That night, Henry asked Lady Castleton to introduce him to Caro. Despite his best efforts, however,
the little bride proved stubbornly resistant to his seductive techniques. Her declaration that she would
always be faithful to her husband had sent him grimly
back to Lady Roxley.

When Henry entered her sitting-room, she was again
at her bonheur du jour.

As she rose to greet him, he told her angrily, 'Your
plan is all to pieces. The bride refuses to be
compromised.'

Lady Roxley shrugged. 'That does not matter in
the least, thanks to Lady Lewis. Now, Henry, here is
what you must do.'

Returning from her morning ride with Sam, her
groom, Caro was surprised to see Ashley's travelling
coach stopped in front of Bourn House. He had said
nothing to her about making a journey. Hurrying
inside, she found Mercer Corte in the hall with her
husband. Caro asked Ashley whether he was going
away.

'Merce and I are journeying to Brighton.'

Feeling bereft at the prospect of London without
her husband, she asked, 'When will you return?'

'Late tomorrow at the earliest, but I may be gone
for two or three days.' His eyes were sombre. 'I wish
to be private with you for a moment. Step into the
book-room with me.'

Much alarmed by his demeanour, Caro complied.
As he shut the door behind them, she said anxiously,
'You look as though someone has died.'

'Someone has, but it was some months ago.'

'I don't understand.'

Instead of explaining, he said without preamble, 'Despite my wishes, you have continued to flirt with Henry. Please believe me, elfin, when I tell you that it is only your welfare that concerns me. I did not ask you to stay away from him because I was jealous of him—for I am not—but because I believe he means to do you harm.'

'What nonsense!' Caro scoffed. 'Why would he want to do that?'

'If my father and I die before I produce a male heir, the Bourn title and estate would go to Henry. If you were to become pregnant, the child would stand between him and that inheritance.'

Caro gasped. 'Surely you cannot think that Henry...'

'I think that Henry killed my brother. However, I lack proof, which I think can be supplied by a man named Chester Moking. I have been searching for him in vain for weeks now. This morning I received word that he is in Brighton. That is why I journey there. Mercer is going with me because he has twice seen Moking and can identify him.'

Caro stared at her husband in disbelief. 'Henry cannot be a killer!'

'You are too trusting, Caro,' Ashley said grimly. 'Before I leave, I want you to give me your word that you will have nothing more to do with Henry.'

'I will not do so,' she said flatly. 'I find your suspicions ridiculous.'

'Do not be such a naïve, soft-hearted little fool!' Ashley exclaimed in exasperation.

Stung, she cried, 'I am not a fool!'

'You are, if you trust Henry.' Ashley's voice was low and urgent. 'Now, give me your word that you will have nothing more to do with him.'

'No,' she said stubbornly, certain that Henry would never harm her.

'Your word, Caro. Now!' her husband snapped, his patience with her clearly at an end. 'You are delaying Merce and me. If you do not stop acting like a wilful, foolish child, I shall be forced to treat you like one by locking you in your room while I am gone. Which will it be?'

Caro knew from the hard set of his face that he would do what he threatened. He looked for all the world like a stern father dealing with an unruly daughter. Although she was furious at him for treating her like this, she could not tolerate the embarrassment of being confined to her room. Sullenly, she capitulated, mumbling, 'I give you my word.'

His penetrating green eyes examined her silently for a moment, as though he were trying to decide whether she would keep it. The fact that he could doubt her word, no matter how reluctantly given, further fuelled her anger.

Finally he said softly, 'Thank you, elfin.' He put his hands on her arms and would have kissed her, but Caro, still seething, pushed him away, saying coldly, 'I do not wish to delay you and Mercer any further.'

Ashley looked as though she had slapped him. He turned on his heel and stalked from the room. A moment later, she heard the front door close behind him and Mercer, then the sound of the carriage moving off.

A sudden thought doused Caro's anger like a dash of ice-water. If Henry had killed William to remove him from the succession, her husband, too, was in grave danger.

'Oh, Ashley, be careful. I love you so,' she admitted to the silent room. 'I could not bear to lose you.'

CHAPTER TWENTY-SIX

WHEN Caro, dressed in a forest-green riding-habit and a matching high-crowned hat with a jaunty ostrich feather in its band, went to claim her horse the following morning for her ride in the park, she was surprised to see a stranger, instead of her usual groom, holding the reins of her hack.

'Where is Sam?' she asked.

'Oi'm told 'e's under the weather, ma'am,' the man answered.

'What's wrong with him?' Caro cried, immediately concerned.

'Oi don't know, ma'am,' his replacement replied, looking uneasy. He had a pockmarked face, a slovenly carriage and an unkempt look about him that surprised Caro, for her husband required the servants who wore his burgundy and gold livery to present an impeccable appearance. But this man's livery was ill-fitting, as though it were a size too small. Caro decided that he must be a stableboy who had been hastily pressed into service because of Sam's illness.

Caro loved this time of day. There was hardly anyone about on the streets except for a mounted butcher-boy making deliveries. His saddle had a tray for his wares strapped on to its front and only one stirrup, but he managed to ride at a bruising pace despite these hindrances.

When Caro and her groom reached the park, it was all but deserted of humanity. Cows and deer browsed peacefully beneath the trees and along paths that in the late afternoon would become congested with the carriages of the ton.

Caro had stayed at home the previous night. The entertainments on her schedule did not tempt her when she knew in advance that she would not see Ashley at any of them. Nor had she any interest in seeing Henry Neel. Not that she could bring herself to believe he was a murderer. But when she had learned the real reason that Ashley objected to her flirtation with his cousin, it had effectively killed what small interest he had held for her.

She turned her hack down her favourite path, the one she chose every morning for its quiet seclusion. It was guarded on both sides by tall thick hedgerows of guelder rose, elder and black bryony. A nondescript closed carriage, without a crest on the door or a coachman on the box, was parked off the side of the path in a secluded little nook. How strange, Caro thought, slowing her mount to a walk as she passed it. This was the first time she had seen a vehicle on this path during her morning rides. Even stranger, it appeared to be abandoned.

Suddenly her groom called to her to halt. 'Oi needs to check yer cinch. Methinks it's loose.'

Although Caro had noticed no problem with it, she obediently stopped and dismounted.

Her feet were barely on the ground when she sensed a movement in the bushes behind her. A dark shroud descended over her head and she was enveloped in its scratchy, mouldy-smelling folds. Before she could recover from her surprise, a rope was looped about the outside of the blanket and pulled tight round her arms, binding them to her sides. A second rope was applied in like manner to her ankles.

Caro tried to scream, but the thick material muffled the sound. Not that there would be anyone about in the park at this hour to hear her. Suddenly she was hoisted off her feet, thrown over a burly shoulder, and carried off as though she were a sack of grain.

A minute later, she was unceremoniously tossed into a vehicle—no doubt the closed carriage she had seen—and dumped on the seat, still tied in the rough blanket. She tried to struggle against her bonds but quickly realised that this was futile. She was as helpless as a trussed goose. The coach started up and was soon moving at a lively pace.

Although terrified, Caro refused to give in to panic, despite being scarcely able to breathe through the scratchy blanket's thick folds. She should have been more suspicious of that unkempt groom who most certainly must be part of the kidnapping plot. But who would want to abduct her and why?

'Who are you?' she demanded. 'What do you want?'

There was no response, and she could not be certain that her abductors even heard her question through the blanket. Its wretched smell made her gag. An unnerving thought struck her. It was just like being wrapped in a shroud preparatory to being laid in a grave.

The wheels of the coach left the dirt of the park's paths for the hard cobblestones of a London street, where costermongers' cries advertising their wares were already being heard. Caro tried to scream again, but the effort was drowned in the blanket's folds, the clatter of metal wheels on stone and the din of pedlars' cries.

Several minutes later, the carriage stopped. Caro, still in her black shroud, was again picked up and tossed over the burly shoulder. This time she was carried a short distance before her captor climbed a long flight of stairs that, she perceived from the turns he made, must have several landings. At last she was dropped on her backside on the floor.

The sharp blade of a knife cut the rope that bound her arms, then the one round her feet, and the blanket was thrown off her. After the darkness, her eyes were blinded by the sudden light that assaulted them, and she could bring the room into focus only slowly.

Raising herself to a sitting position, she saw that she was in a handsomely decorated bedchamber, clearly a man's from the masculine furnishings, which included a mahogany armoire, a sturdy round table with a porcelain ewer and basin, and a four-drawer mahogany dressing-chest with a serpentine front. The room was dominated by a large tester bed with a flat canopy and a petticoat valance. Although it was the time of day to be getting up rather than retiring, its red coverlet was pulled back and its pillows plumped up in preparation for occupants.

The room had but one door, and a broad, hulking man in coarse clothes, his pants held up by a rope tied round his waist, was moving towards it. From his size, Caro knew that he had to be the man who had carried her up the stairs. He was followed out of the door by her substitute groom. A third man in a

brocade dressing-gown was standing beside the door
with his back to her. He told the groom, 'First, bring
up the chocolate, Needham. Then get out of that livery
and bury it. Be quick about it. Lord Oldfield and
Plymtree arrive here in an hour.'

Caro recognised Henry Neel's voice. He pushed the
door closed, leaving her alone in the bedchamber with
him, turned the key in the lock, and dropped it into
his pocket.

Fear prickled along Caro's spine. She had thought
her husband's concern for her safety at Henry's hand
silly, but now she knew that Ashley had been right.
Determined not to let Henry see her fear, she
scrambled to her feet, demanding, 'What is the
meaning of this?'

He laughed. 'I desire your company, my dear.'

'It is an odd way you have of obtaining it,' she said
tartly. 'Be so kind as to restore me to my home.'

'I shall, in due course.'

'Do so immediately!' Hiding her desperation beneath a haughty veneer, she lied, 'My husband is
expecting me home to breakfast with him.'

Henry laughed harshly. 'Your husband is in
Brighton.'

'How do you know?' Caro gasped.

'Because I was responsible for sending him there in
search of the one-eared man who is nowhere in the
vicinity.'

'Why? To get him out of town while you abduct
me?'

'You have a quick understanding.'

'But why have you abducted me?'

The cold hardness of his eyes frightened her. 'I have an insatiable desire to bed you. Much as it grieves my consequence as a notorious seducer to admit it, I did not think you could be persuaded to come to it any other way.'

Nausea roiled in Caro's stomach. 'You mean to rape me?'

'Nothing so crude as that, I assure you. In truth, I prefer my women considerably more, shall we say, voluptuous than you, my dear. I merely wish for you to occupy my bed for a little while.'

'And then?'

'And then I will send you home.'

For a moment she stared at him, perplexed. Then, remembering what he had said about Lord Oldfield, the nastiest gossip in all of London, and Plymtree coming to call, comprehension dawned. 'You mean your visitors to find us together.'

'As I said, you have a quick understanding. Plymtree, who dislikes you intensely, will be particularly edified to see you in my bed and only too delighted to spread the word of your infidelity.' Henry smiled at her wickedly. 'We shall be the scandal of London, my dear.'

Caro reeled beneath the impact of his words and grabbed one of the bedposts to steady herself. *I will not tolerate a wife who involves me or my name in a scandal!* Ashley would certainly divorce her now. No longer able to hide her emotion, her voice cracked as she asked, 'How will my ruin obtain the earldom for you?'

Her question clearly startled him. 'Good God, is that what your husband thinks: that I am after the title? No, he can rest easy on that score.'

'Then why did you kill William?'

'Did you ever meet your husband's brother?'

'No.'

'You were fortunate. He was the most sanctimonious, overbearing, toplofty bastard I ever met.'

'You did not like him,' Caro observed politely.

'I loathed him as much as he loathed me. The pompous cod'shead thought himself so much better than he was, particularly when it came to tooling the ribbons. I wanted nothing so much as to see him and all his consequence in the dust.'

'So you murdered him.'

'It was his pride, not his body, that I sought to wound. I meant only for him to suffer a humiliating defeat in that accurst race, but William, disobliging as always, caught a congestion of the lungs and died. I will not permit him the last laugh by sending me to the gallows. That is why you are here, my dear.'

'The connection escapes me,' Caro said.

'You are only a means to my end of silencing your husband's lips on the subject of his brother's death. He means to see me convicted of it. After today, however, he will think twice before he publicly accuses me of murdering William.'

'I still do not understand.'

'You disappoint me, but your husband will grasp it immediately. No matter how long and hard he tries, he will find no proof of my involvement in his brother's death, because there is none. The best he can hope for is the word of a disreputable associate of mine. Vinson can make the accusation, but he would be a fool to do so after today.'

'Why?'

'Only think how very peculiar it will look that he waited so many months after his brother's death to lodge the charge, doing so only after my seduction of his bride had become the talk of London. Nothing is more humiliating to a man than to have the world know that he has been cuckolded. I will be able to laugh off his allegation as nothing more than a crude attempt to revenge himself on me. By accusing me, he will only intensify the scandal over his faithless wife.'

Caro's hands covered her mouth in horror and despair at Henry's scheme. 'Ashley will divorce me,' she moaned.

Henry smiled cruelly. 'Very likely. He married you only for an heir, which a faithless wife is no longer worthy of bearing.'

'You are mad if you think I will not trumpet your abduction of me at the top of my lungs.'

'Of course you will,' he agreed. 'Just as Lady Lewis did. And after her Banbury tale, you will have even less chance than she of being believed. Everyone will think that you are borrowing her story in a desperate effort to cover your guilt.'

'You are diabolical!' Caro cried, her voice trembling with loathing. 'Are you so certain that Oldfield and Plymtree will believe you instead of me when they find us?'

Henry only gave her a triumphant little smile that made her flesh crawl. Somehow he was certain that this would be the case. There was more to his plan than he had told her.

Suddenly he jerked off her hat, its high crown and once perky feather now sadly crushed, and tossed it casually on the dressing-chest.

'Don't you touch me!' she cried in revulsion.

'Then you must oblige me by removing your riding-habit and getting into my bed.'

'I will do no such thing!'

Before she realised what he was about, his quick hands seized the front of her habit and ripped it open to her waist, sending its black jet buttons flying in all directions.

'If you do as I say, I shall permit you to retain your shift,' Henry told her. 'Otherwise, I shall have the pleasure of stripping you naked.'

Staring into his hard face, Caro knew that he would do exactly as he threatened and that he was far too strong for her to fight off. A red flush of shame coloured her face at the thought of being naked in front of his cruel, mocking eyes. 'Very well,' she said with as much dignity as she could muster.

A knock sounded at the door. Henry crossed to it, pulled the key from his pocket, and unlocked it. Needham entered, carrying a tray with a cup of chocolate and a slice of toast on it. Caro hastily turned her back to him so that he could not see her torn habit.

'Set it on the table beside the bed, Needham,' Henry instructed. 'I'll join you downstairs in a few minutes. Be sure you are out of that livery by then.'

Needham left, and Henry relocked the door. 'Now get undressed and into bed,' he told Caro.

'Turn your back,' she demanded.

He shrugged and did so. Hastily shedding her riding-habit, she climbed beneath the bedcovers and pulled them up to her chin before Henry could turn round and see her in her shift.

'Drink your chocolate,' he told her.

Her stomach convulsed at the thought. 'I don't want it.'

'Drink it, I said,' he snapped at her.

Caro stiffened with alarm, looking dubiously at the cup of chocolate. Had he borrowed another leaf from Lady Lewis's story and drugged her chocolate? 'My stomach is unsettled. I fear it will make me sick.'

'Drink it, or I'll pour it down your damn throat!' he said, taking a step towards her.

'No, please, I'll drink it,' she agreed, reaching for the cup, certain now that its contents were drugged. No wonder Henry had no concern about Oldfield and Plymtree disbelieving him. They would find her dead asleep beside Henry in his bed. Later, if she tried to cry that she had been abducted and drugged, no one would believe her story, especially not coming on the heels of Lady Lewis's Banbury tale.

Caro tried frantically to think of some way to escape. She brought the cup to her face, sniffing its contents as she simultaneously raised her knees to her chest. There was an odd, bitter odour to the chocolate that made her more certain than ever that it was tainted.

'Hurry up and drink it,' Henry ordered.

'Yes, I will, but I feel so unwell. Please bring me that basin in case I cast up my accounts after drinking it. I should not like to ruin your coverlet.'

Henry muttered an angry oath but, nevertheless, turned and went to get the basin. The instant his back was turned, Caro, lifted the coverlet and dumped the contents of the cup on to the bed beneath her raised legs. Hastily she returned the cup to her lips. When Henry turned towards her with the basin, she appeared to be gulping its contents.

Then she made a face. 'What odd-tasting chocolate,' she said, replacing the cup on the tray.

The evil smile her words brought to his lips sent shivers down her spine. When a couple of minutes had passed, Caro yawned and said sleepily, 'I do not believe I need the basin. I am suddenly so tired and groggy. All I want to do is to sleep.' She slid down beneath the coverlet, forcing herself to keep from grimacing as she felt the sticky chocolate beneath her, and pretended to drift off to sleep.

After a couple of minutes, Henry called softly, 'Caro, Caro, are you awake?'

She pretended that she was not. He picked up her wrist and she let it fall like a dead weight. He lifted it again and shook it lightly. Still receiving no response, he muttered. 'She'll be out cold until long after Oldfield and Plymtree have left.' He let her wrist drop on to the mattress. 'Sleep well, my Lady Vinson. I shall join you after I have finished my preparations for our guests.'

Caro heard him cross the room and go out of the door. Then the key turned, locking it from the outside. Her heart sank. She had counted on his neglecting to lock the door. She had planned to slip out while he was gone and escape before Oldfield and Plymtree arrived. Once they saw her, whether they believed her story or not, there would be a dreadful scandal, and Ashley would surely divorce her.

Somehow she had to get out before she was seen in Henry's house. Throwing back the covers, she jumped out of bed. Her only other hope lay in climbing out of one of the two long windows. A quick inspection, however, discouraged her. The room was at the back of the house on the second floor. Caro gulped as she saw how heart-stoppingly far down the ground was.

And there was not a tree in sight. She was trapped.

CHAPTER TWENTY-SEVEN

ASHLEY'S travelling carriage was moving at a speed that most would have considered foolhardy in crowded London streets.

'Must we continue at this breakneck pace?' Mercer Corte complained. 'Curzon Street is just ahead. I am confident that this wild-goose chase we have been sent on signifies nothing more than an attempt to collect the reward you offered for information about Chester Moking's whereabouts.'

'I wish that I could share your confidence, but I cannot,' Ashley replied glumly, his fingers drumming impatiently on his knee as he reviewed the events of the previous twenty-four hours. First, there had been the appearance at Bourn House of a rough, burly individual dressed in shabby pants held up by a rope. The visitor would be happy to tell m'lord where Chester Moking could be found if m'lord would but hand over the reward he had offered.

In retrospect, m'lord should have been suspicious when the caller put up no strong argument to being paid only a tenth of the money until Ashley could make certain that Moking was indeed at the Blue Moon Inn in Brighton, as the informer said.

'Never heard of a Blue Moon Inn in Brighton,' Ashley had said.

The man had replied jovially, 'Not a ken a swell like yer'd 'ave heard a.'

Nor, as it turned out, had anyone else heard of it, for it did not exist.

At first, Vinson had been inclined to accept Mercer's theory that the man had merely been trying to bilk him out of the offered reward. But the more Ashley thought about it, the more certain he became that his trip to Brighton had been a ruse planned by his cousin to get him out of town. But why? The only possible answer was that Henry had some evil scheme afoot involving Caro and wanted her husband out of the way while he executed it.

After several sleepless hours, the Viscount, growing increasingly convinced that his wife was in danger, had risen and insisted that they return to London at once.

They had set out before dawn. A yawning Mercer Corte, disgruntled at being dragged from bed at such an ungoldly hour, had asked, 'But what could Henry possibly do to Caro?'

This question had plagued Ashley all the way to London. The ride seemed interminable, but at last his carriage was turning down Curzon Street and home was in sight.

Looking out of the window, Mercer said, ''Tis shocking what one sees on even the best streets these days. Look at that sorry creature, barefoot and wrapped in a blanket.'

Ashley glanced out. Recognising the derelict as Caro's groom, Sam, he shouted for the coachman to stop. Even before the carriage rolled to a halt, Ashley leaped out and ran up to Sam, who appeared to be wearing little else but the blanket. 'Where are your clothes?'

The groom blenched at the sight of his master, and dropped his eyes in embarrassment. 'Stolen, milord.'

'What happened?' Ashley demanded tersely, certain that his worst fears were being confirmed.

Sam related how he had gone, as was his custom, for a pint at a nearby alehouse the previous night. A stranger had sat down beside him and been very friendly, eventually insisting on buying him a second pint. Sam remembered nothing after drinking it until he awoke this morning with an aching head in a back alley of St Giles. His clothes and shoes were gone, and he had been forced to barter his ring for the blanket he was wrapped in. Then he had set out on the long walk to Curzon Street.

'Prigged your livery, but left your ring,' Ashley observed grimly.

'Odd,' Sam agreed. 'What can they have thought to gain by taking it?'

'My wife.' Ashley broke into a run for Bourn House, a little way away. As he burst inside, Boothe and Caro's maid Hélène were worriedly conferring.

'Where is my wife?'

'My lady has not returned from her morning ride,' Boothe said.

Ashley dashed back outside as his carriage pulled up. He jumped on the box beside his startled coachman and took the reins. If the carriage's pace to Curzon Street had been breakneck, its speed now was positively suicidal as Ashley guided it skilfully through the traffic, swerving to miss other vehicles and cursing pedestrians.

Inside the coach, Mercer Corte could be heard enquiring in pungent terms whether Ashley was a raving

lunatic or merely touched in the upper works. Even
the Viscount's coachman, who was known for his steel
nerves, closed his eyes and appeared to be praying
fervently as the equipage raced towards Chesterfield
Street.

Caro stared at the long drop from Henry's bedroom
window to the ground. She felt as though she were
staring over the edge of a precipice from which there
was no escape.

She tried to summon up her failing courage, but
her good sense told her it was far too dangerous to
attempt to escape via this route. However, if she did
not get away before Oldfield and Plymtree saw her in
Henry's bedroom, she would be ruined by the en-
suing scandal, and lose her husband in the bargain.
*Take care, Caro! I will not tolerate a wife who in-
volves me or my name in a scandal!*

Would Ashley think that she had gone willingly to
his cousin's bed? Her heart seemed to shatter into a
thousand fragments at the thought of Ashley casting
her off.

She eyed the window with renewed determination.
It was the only possible way of escaping before
Oldfield and Plymtree saw her. Trying to pump up
her courage, she recalled how she had climbed down
from her room at Aunt Olive's without the assistance
of a tree. But there the distance to the ground had
not been nearly so great. She would be a fool to try
this drop.

But if she did not, she would lose Ashley.

All other concerns receded before that paramount
one. It propelled Caro to the bed. Quickly she stripped

the linen and blankets, frantically knotting them together in a colourful, makeshift rope. When she finished, she tied one end around the leg of the armoire,
then retrieved her clothes.

Unfortunately they were hardly suitable for climbing
out of upper-storey windows. Caro hastily donned her
skirt and, with shaking fingers, tied it up about her
thighs to keep it from hampering her descent down
the rope. Her modesty rebelled at the thought of the
view anyone standing on the ground below would
have. But this was the back of the house, and no one
would be there, so why was she worrying?

Her modesty suffered another jolt when she put on
the top of her riding-habit. With the buttons ripped
away, she had no way to fasten it. She could hardly
flee unnoticed through the streets of London with her
bodice gaping open. Hurrying to the armoire, she
searched through the garments that were stored there
and selected a man's black wool cloak.

Caro dropped it to the ground beneath the window,
then lowered the makeshift rope. She gulped when
she saw that its end dangled several feet short of the
ground. She would have to drop the rest of the way!

Leaning over the window-ledge, Caro gripped it
with white-knuckled fingers as she stared to the ground
so far beneath. She struggled vainly to conquer the
fear that paralysed her now that the moment of action
was at hand. Did she have the courage to go through
with this mad attempt?

Thinking again of Ashley, she forced herself to
climb up on the window-ledge. Grasping the bedclothes in both hands, she slowly began her perilous

descent, inching her way down, her feet braced against the wall.

Her arms soon ached from the unaccustomed strain on them. By the time she was half-way down, she strongly doubted that her tortured limbs would continue to function until she could reach the ground, still so far beneath her. She dared not look down for fear her courage would fail her. Instead, she concentrated on the brick wall and on forcing her reluctant hands and arms, weak with exhaustion, to perform their agonising task.

Finally, after what seemed like hours, she reached the end of the makeshift rope and found that her feet were still well off the ground.

Suddenly, without warning, strong arms seized her from behind, encircling her hips. She was so shocked and terrified that her numb hands fell away from the improvised rope she was clutching and her heart seemed to explode in her chest. A groan of despair was wrenched from her. Her tortuous descent had been in vain. Henry had caught her!

Her captor lowered her feet to the ground, saying harshly, 'You little idiot!'

Caro gasped at the sound of Ashley's furious voice. Where had he come from? He forced her round to face him. His expression, already deadly, turned murderous when he saw her torn riding-habit. She had never seen him so angry, and her heart sank. He would never believe her queer tale.

'I am torn between wanting to wring that foolish neck of yours,' he ground out, 'and giving thanks that I caught you before you could break it.'

'I wish I had broken it,' she said miserably. All that she had been through that day—the abduction, her terrifying descent from the upper-storey window, and now the knowledge that Ashley was irrevocably lost to her—was too much for her to bear, and she began to sob in despair.

With a violent curse, Ashley snatched up the black cloak that she had dropped to the ground and wrapped it round her. Swinging her up into his arms, he carried her through a passage that ran along the side of Henry's house to the street in front, where Mercer Corte was waiting beside the Viscount's carriage.

Ashley thrust her inside, saying roughly to Mercer, 'Take her to Bourn House.'

Mercer jumped into the carriage, and it began to move immediately.

'No,' Caro cried desperately, 'Ashley, please come with me.'

But he had turned his back. If he heard her, he gave no sign of it. Then the carriage turned the corner, and he vanished from her sight.

And, no doubt, from her life as well.

CHAPTER TWENTY-EIGHT

NEEDHAM, in the dress of one of Henry Neel's servants, appeared before his employer with the livery that had been stolen from Vinson's groom wrapped in a bundle.

Henry gestured at it. 'Burn that at once. We cannot risk its being found here. You know what you are to do when Oldfield and Plymtree arrive. I must depend on you, because I have given my servants the day off.'

'Never do to 'ave 'em spoiling yer game,' Needham agreed. 'Yer only worry's the lady's reaction to yer visitors.'

'She is so drugged she won't even know that they are there,' Henry replied.

A loud banging at the front door echoed through the house.

'Damn! Oldfield and Plymtree are here already,' Henry cried, glancing at the longcase clock. 'I've never known either of them to be less than a half-hour late, and now they are ten minutes early. Give me time to get upstairs, then let them in. You know what to tell them, then bring them up to my bedroom.'

Henry dashed up the stairs, unfastening the sash of his dressing-gown as he ran. At the door to his room, he had to fumble in his pocket for the key, and cursed himself for not having left it in the lock. Finally, though, he extracted it. As he opened the door, he heard a strangled shout from Needham, then a loud

crash. But his attention was riveted to his bed, which
had been stripped bare to its mattress. He looked
frantically about the room. Caro was nowhere in sight.
Then Henry saw the rope of bedclothes hanging over
the window-sill. For a moment he was too stunned to
move. The little fool must be lying dead beneath his
window.

There was no way that he could explain that. He
reeled with shock at how badly his—or more precisely, Lady Roxley's—scheme had backfired. Now
he would be accused of two deaths, not just one.
When Ashley discovered that his cousin was responsible for his wife's death, he would not rest until he
saw him ride the three-legged mare.

A loud crash on the first floor, followed by footsteps running up the stairs, brought Henry back to
the present. The steps were too light and quick to be
Needham's. Neel fled toward the back stairs. As he
reached them, he turned and saw Vinson running
down the hall towards him.

With the spectre of the gallows shadowing him,
Henry fled down the stairs and through the dark hall
to a door that opened at the front of the house below
street level.

As he burst through the door and up the stairs that
led to the street, a groom was trying to control a black
stallion, young and high-strung, that pawed nervously at the paving-stones in front of an impressive
mansion surrounded by tall iron palings.

'Stop!' Ashley was calling, his voice close behind
Henry. 'You can't escape me.'

Desperate, Henry raced up to the stallion, snatched
the reins from the startled groom and leaped into the

saddle. The horse, frightened by this sudden man-
oeuvre and by unfamiliar hands on the reins, reared
violently. Henry managed to stay on, but then the
horse reared again and again. Henry felt as though
he were trying to hang on to a lightning-bolt. Then
suddenly he was flying through the air towards the
iron palings.

At Bourn House, Caro, still sobbing, was undressed
and bundled into bed by Hélène, who had drawn the
curtains and tried to give her young mistress something to make her sleep. But Caro refused it, determined to remain awake until Ashley returned. She
must try to counteract the lies that Henry would be
telling her husband even now.

Finally, her door opened and Ashley came in. Caro
sat up as her husband crossed to her. In the flickering
light of the single candle that Hélène had left burning
beside the bed, his face was as grim as she had ever
seen it. Hope, which had leaped at the sight of him,
crumbled into dust when she saw his expression.

Shivering, she pulled the bedclothes up to her neck
as though to protect herself from his furious gaze,
which she met with despairing eyes.

'What did Henry do to you?' he demanded.

Why, she wondered dully, was Ashley bothering to
ask her when he had already heard Henry's lies and
no doubt believed them? 'What did he tell you that
he did?' she asked listlessly.

'I am asking you, Caro. Did, he, er, touch you?'

'He tore the buttons from my riding-habit,' she said
dully, 'and he threatened to force a cup of drugged
chocolate down my throat.'

'That is not what I mean.'

A flush spread over Caro's face as she comprehended what he did mean. 'No, not that way.' She could not keep a trace of bitterness from her voice. 'Like my husband, Henry prefers more voluptuous women. You were right when you told me that he was not interested in me. He wanted only to create a scandal. What did he tell you? That he had seduced me?'

Ashley, his face troubled, sat down on the bed beside her. 'He told me nothing. He is dead.'

Caro was shocked out of her lethargy. 'You killed him?'

'No, although God knows I wanted to when I saw you coming down that makeshift rope. I felt as though I lived a dozen lifetimes before you descended far enough for me to reach you. I went after Henry with murder in my heart for what he had put you through. He tried to escape from me by stealing a horse.' Ashley passed a weary hand over his eyes as if he were trying to erase a terrible scene from his mind. 'It threw him, and he was impaled on a fence. That is why I have been gone so long. There were a great many questions to answer.'

'And now there will be a dreadful scandal,' Caro said bitterly. 'Will you divorce me?'

'What?' he asked blankly.

'You said that you would not tolerate a wife who involved you in scandal.'

'Caro, no one will know that you were at Henry's house today. I have seen to that. If there is any scandal, it will be over Henry's responsibility for my brother's death.'

'Henry did not want the title,' Caro said. 'He told me that he did not mean to kill your brother, only to humiliate him by making him lose the race, but that William disobligingly took ill and died.'

'Oh, God,' Ashley groaned. 'So that was it. What a damnable waste!' He shook his head sadly. 'I cannot blame my cousin for hating William. He treated Henry so contemptuously.'

'I did not go to your cousin's house,' Caro said, certain that her husband would never believe her improbable tale. 'He abducted me.'

'Yes, I know. Poor elfin.'

'You believe me?' Caro's voice quavered in surprise and relief.

'Of course. You had given me your word, and I knew that, no matter how reluctantly you did so, you would never go back on it.' Gathering her in his arms, Ashley lifted her on to his lap and hugged her to him. 'Now, tell me what happened.'

When she had finished her story, her husband's arms tightened round her as though he never meant to let her go, and he said fervently, 'You were very brave, elfin, but I would have infinitely preferred a scandal to your risking that lovely little neck of yours by climbing down from the window.'

Tears glistened in her eyes. 'But you would have divorced me!'

He brushed her tears away gently with his thumbs. 'And you do not want that?' he asked softly, his eyes grave.

'No!' She could no longer hide her feelings from him. Her arms tightened around him. 'Oh, Ashley, I love you so much.'

His lips descended on hers in a long, fierce kiss that left them breathless.

'If you love me so, elfin, why have you held me at such a distance in recent weeks?' The baffled hurt in Ashley's voice made Caro wince. 'You acted as though you preferred the company of every other man in London to mine.'

For the first time, it occurred to Caro that her behaviour had wounded as well as puzzled him. 'I wanted your company desperately,' she confessed, 'but I did not want to be like Lady Yarwood and embarrass you by hanging on you when you cannot love me.'

He looked shocked. 'Whoever gave you the nonsensical idea that I don't love you, elfin? Or that I prefer more voluptuous women?'

Caro, remembering what he had told Lady Roxley, could not suppress two large tears that rolled down her cheeks. 'You did.'

His hands tightened round her arms. 'What the devil are you talking about?'

'I cannot tell you.'

'Why not?'

Caro hung her head. 'I would be breaking my word that I will not vex you about your mistress.'

'Since I do not have a mistress, you cannot vex me about her and, therefore, you cannot break your word,' he said roughly.

'Oh, Ashley, don't try to gammon me,' she cried, the aching of her heart echoed in her voice. 'I know the truth. I overheard you tell Lady Roxley that she need never worry that I would steal your love from her.'

Her husband swore softly, his face tightening into grim, angry lines. 'And, hearing that much, you ran away, didn't you?'

'Yes,' she said miserably, wondering how he knew that. 'I could not bear to hear any more.'

'You would have saved us both a great deal of misery had you stayed to hear me to the end. What I told my *former* mistress was that she need not worry that you *would* replace her in my affections because you *already had* done so.'

For a moment, Caro could only stare at him in disbelief. 'Truly?'

'Truly, elfin.'

But she was still sceptical. 'How can you possibly love me instead of Lady Roxley? She is so beautiful.'

'Believe me, elfin, it is very easy. She is a faithless, selfish creature, but it took me a long time to see beyond her beauty and manipulative charm.'

Still Caro would not let herself succumb to the happiness that was welling in her. 'But you did not love me when you married me.'

'No,' Ashley admitted. 'We had known each other less than a fortnight. But I was very fond of you. Once we were married, affection quickly deepened into love. But it took me a while to realise that. It was not until I went back to Bellhaven and saw you running so eagerly to greet me that I knew that I had lost my heart to you.'

'Oh, Ashley,' she breathed, 'why did you not tell me that you loved me?'

'I thought that I did, although not in words, perhaps, each time we made love.' His hand caressed the curve of her hip resting on his lap. 'The nights have been so lonely for me without you beside me. Did you miss me, too?'

'Too much,' she confessed, embarrassment tinting her cheeks as she remembered her wild, unladylike response that had so shocked him. Now, more than ever, she wanted to be exactly the kind of wife he wanted.

'What do you mean, "too much"?' he asked gently, lifting her chin so that he could look into her eyes.

'You drive me wild,' she answered candidly, 'and when you do, I cannot, no matter how hard I try, act like a lady of the first respectability.'

Ashley's eyes gleamed with laughter. 'Elfin, a man does not want a lady of the first respectability in bed.'

'Even if she is his wife?'

'Especially if she is his wife.'

'What does he want?'

His mouth came down, hovering over hers. 'A woman like you, my elfin.'

THREE TOP NOVELS –
A GREAT READING SELECTION

DILEMMA – Megan Alexander £2.50

With her future all mapped out, Shannon Gallagher hadn't counted on the dilemma she now faced – the return of her ex-husband, which threatened to change the tender memories of the past into a living nightmare.

WHISPER IN THE WIND – Ann Hulme £2.95

In the sequel to her bestselling novel *The Flying Man*, Ann Hulme poignantly depicts the contrasts of World War II – the tragedy, the danger, the sadness and the snatched moments of lovers destined to wait for what the future holds.

THE WHOLE TRUTH – Jenny Loring £2.75

The compelling novel of a woman at the top of the career ladder. As a respected judge, Susannah Ross faces a case which could compromise her entire career.

These three new titles will be out in bookshops from June 1989.

W RLDWIDE

Available from Boots, Martins, John Menzies, W. H. Smith, Woolworths and other paperback stockists.

COMING SOON FROM MILLS & BOON!

Your chance to win the fabulous

VAUXHALL ASTRA
MERIT 1.2 5-DOOR

Plus

**2000 RUNNER UP PRIZES OF WEEKEND
BREAKS & CLASSIC LOVE SONGS ON CASSETTE**

♥ SEE
MILLS & BOON BOOKS
THROUGHOUT JULY & AUGUST FOR DETAILS! ♥

Offer available through Boots, Martins, John Menzies, WH Smith,
Woolworths and all good paperback stockists in the UK, Eire and Overseas.

AROUND THE WORLD WORDSEARCH
COMPETITION!

How would you like a years supply of Mills & Boon Romances ABSOLUTELY FREE? Well, you can win them! All you have to do is complete the word puzzle below and send it in to us by October 31st. 1989. The first 5 correct entries picked out of the bag after that date will win **a years supply of Mills & Boon Romances** (*ten books every month - **worth around £150***) What could be easier?

R	D	N	A	L	R	E	Z	T	I	W	S
E	O	N	M	C	H	I	N	A	A	C	C
G	M	U	I	G	L	E	B	N	N	U	O
Y	E	C	E	G	W	H	I	Z	C	B	T
P	D	R	H	S	E	R	I	A	Z	A	L
T	N	S	M	P	E	R	U	N	D	D	A
N	A	W	I	A	T	P	I	I	E	N	N
Y	L	A	T	I	N	A	N	A	N	A	D
N	G	S	T	N	H	Y	D	E	M	L	Q
W	N	O	J	A	M	A	I	C	A	L	A
R	E	L	A	D	A	N	A	C	R	O	R
T	H	A	I	L	A	N	D	D	K	H	I

ITALY	THAILAND	SCOTLAND	SWITZERLAND
GERMANY	IRAQ	JAMAICA	
HOLLAND	ZAIRE	TANZANIA	**PLEASE TURN**
BELGIUM	TAIWAN	PERU	**OVER FOR**
EGYPT	CANADA	SPAIN	**DETAILS**
CHINA	INDIA	DENMARK	**ON HOW**
NIGERIA	ENGLAND	CUBA	**TO ENTER**

HOW TO ENTER

All the words listed overleaf, below the word puzzle, are hidden in the grid. You can find them by reading the letters forward, backwards, up or down, or diagonally. When you find a word, circle it or put a line through it, the remaining letters (which you can read from left to right, from the top of the puzzle through to the bottom) will spell a secret message.

After you have filled in all the words, don't forget to fill in your name and address in the space provided and pop this page in an envelope (you don't need a stamp) and post it today. Hurry - competition ends October 31st. 1989.

Mills & Boon Competition,
FREEPOST,
P.O. Box 236,
Croydon,
Surrey. CR9 9EL

Only one entry per household

Secret Message _____

_____

Name _____

Address _____

_____

_____

_____ Postcode _____

You may be mailed as a result of entering this competition

COMP 6